# THE GERMAN ROOM

CHARCO PRESS

First published by Charco Press 2018

Charco Press Ltd., Office 59, 44-46 Morningside Road, Edinburgh EH10 4BF

Book published with funding from the 'Sur' Translation Support Programme
of the Ministry of Foreign Affairs of the Republic of Argentina / Obra editada
en el marco del Programa 'Sur' de Apoyo a las Traducciones del Ministerio de
Relaciones Exteriores y Culto de la República Argentina.

ISBN: 978-1-9998593-3-6
e-book: 978-1-9998593-8-1

www.charcopress.com

Edited by Fionn Petch
Cover design by Pablo Font
Typeset by Laura Jones
Proofread by Fiona Mackintosh

2   4   6   8   10   9   7   5   3

Carla Maliandi

# THE GERMAN ROOM

Translated by
Frances Riddle

CHARCO PRESS

# ONE

## I

I once knew the names of all the constellations. My father taught me them, while warning that the German sky above us was totally foreign to him. I was obsessed with the sky, the stars and aeroplanes. I knew that a plane had brought us to Heidelberg and that a plane would take us back to where we belonged. For me, planes had faces and personalities. And I prayed that the one that would take us back to Buenos Aires wasn't one that would fall into the middle of the ocean and kill us all. The night before our trip, our big trip back to Argentina, our house on Keplerstrasse was filled with philosophers. We ate in the garden because it was an unusually warm and clear night. There were some Latin Americans: a Chilean who played the guitar, a serious Mexican philosopher with the requisite beard, and Mario, a young Argentinian student who was staying at our house. The Latin Americans made an effort to speak German and the Germans responded amiably in Spanish. My father argued loudly with a very tall and completely bald philosopher from Frankfurt. At one point they noticed I was frightened and they explained that they weren't fighting, they were just discussing Nicolai Hartmann. When I was a bit older I tried to read Hartmann in order to understand what could've driven them to argue with such passion, but I didn't find anything.

I should sleep now but I can't, I'm still full of nerves from the trip. I look out the window of my new room at a slice of the Heidelberg sky. The last night I was here I stared up at this same sky for a long while trying to memorise it, saying goodbye, storing its image in my mind. The Chilean philosopher played the guitar and began to sing in a gravelly voice 'Gracias a la vida' by Violeta Parra; and all around him the group of enthusiastic, friendly, drunk Germans sang the chorus with ridiculous accents.

How many sleepless nights had I spent in the past month? Yesterday in Buenos Aires I was anxious I wouldn't be ready for the taxi and I kept waking up long before my alarm. When I arrived at the terminal I had a strong coffee to wake me up enough to face the brief airport procedures. On the plane I was dizzy with anxiety again. But this time I wasn't afraid of it falling, I was afraid of landing safe and sound, not knowing what to do or why I was there. Going down with the plane would've been easier than landing in Germany with my life in shambles, without having told anyone in Buenos Aires what I was doing. The prospect of dying on the flight was less terrifying than the thought of riding this surge of impulse to my final destination, without enough money, in a desperate attempt to find peace. And a long-lost happiness, lost and buried forever along with my father. This is not the right way to do things, but it's the way I've done them and here I am. Tomorrow I'll find a phone and call Buenos Aires, and I'll explain as best I can.

I think I'm going to be able to sleep in this place, in this bed. The room is prettier than it had looked online, and I liked everything else the caretaker showed me: the dining hall, the kitchen, and the whole downstairs of the residence. I'm sure it's a great place for a student. But I'm not here to study anything. I'm here to sleep, to get well, and to find a bench in Marktplatz where I can sit and think calmly and eat a pretzel.

## II

I dream that I wake up in a bunk bed inside some kind of pen for humans. Next to me a three-year-old boy sleeps. I wake him up to ask him where we are but the boy doesn't know how to talk. I tell him we have to get out of there. I pick him up and start walking. I'm dressed in the clothes I wore on the plane, a grey sweater and a pair of jeans, but I'm not wearing shoes. The boy is wrapped in a sheet and he's very heavy. We cross a huge pavilion and we crawl under the barbed wire fence that surrounds it. We walk out into a field. There are cows and the ground is covered in fog. Lying under one of the cows is a farmer. He's milking the cow and I can barely see him, he's big and wears lederhosen. When we pass him he offers us a glass of milk. I take the glass and give it to the boy. The man gets mad, he tells me the milk was for me. We argue but we can't understand each other because he speaks with a very strange accent. At one point he looks at my tits, he points to them and I understand perfectly what he's saying: 'There's plenty there for everyone.' I get scared so I take the boy's hand and start to run. As we're running he lets go. I grab him again, and he lets go again, I grab him again and he lets go again. I wake up.

The bed in the residence room is extremely comfortable and I have a window that overlooks a garden. The landscape here is totally different to the devastated field from my dream and the residence exceeds all my expectations as a fake student.

Last night before taking down my details and showing me around, Frau Wittmann, the caretaker, explained that I could make breakfast until nine thirty in the morning. I have to get up right now if I don't want to miss it. Lying in bed I remember my dream and I touch my tits, they're noticeably swollen. I think I must be about to get my period and hope I didn't forget to pack painkillers. I get up, change quickly, run my fingers through my hair, and go down to the dining hall. Students are making coffee and toast. I don't understand the rules, I don't know if I can just grab what I want or if I have to ask permission. It's clear that this isn't a hotel, that no one's going to come and serve me breakfast. Now I understand what Frau Wittmann meant by 'make breakfast'. Everyone is eating something different: toast, yogurt, fruit, or cereal. They take things out of a refrigerator, moving in an orderly fashion, I notice that the things they use have labels with names on them. A line forms around the coffee maker as some students sit talking quietly and others, more solitary, eat breakfast with their notebooks open and don't look at anyone. I feel embarrassed standing here, confused and with messed up hair. I decide to go out for breakfast, just for today.

Heidelberg is like something out of a fairy tale, unreal, one of the few German cities that wasn't bombed. I try to see if I recognise any streets. I spent the first five years of my life here. Some things feel familiar: the bakeries, the Neckar River and its banks, the smell of the streets. It's a warm bright day. I walk inside a storybook, I breathe in deep, I make a game of getting lost in the streets and finding my way again. I go into a café on Marktplatz, I order a breakfast that includes breads, cold meats, orange juice and coffee with milk. The waiter asks me where I'm from, he talks to me about football, he knows the names of all the players from the Argentinian team. I take the opportunity to practice my German. I realise I'm in trouble, that I no longer understand the language very well, that I've forgotten it, that the online lessons I took before coming weren't enough and my good pronunciation doesn't help as much as I'd hoped. As the waiter talks about Messi, I plan my communication strategy. I can speak in English if it doesn't work. I end up resorting to Spanish: '*Sí, Messi es un genio.*' The waiter laughs and goes to check on another table. He leaves repeating: '*Genio, es un genio*'. I wolf down my breakfast, leaving nothing behind. An old man sitting at the next table seems to be eyeing me and I notice that beside his chair is a small dog. The man pets it with one hand and with the other he holds his cup. I estimate his age and wonder what he was doing during the last war. It doesn't matter, even if he's an old Nazi he doesn't have many years left in him. The man suddenly smiles at me. Maybe I'm too quick to judge, he seems like a nice old man. Maybe he could tell I wasn't from here. What do people think when they see me sitting here? I imagine my hair falling limp at my shoulders, the belt I hastily buckled around my waist this morning, the many wrinkles in the pretty shirt I'm wearing. It all seems ridiculous. Ridiculous adornments I use to try and conceal the ruins. No matter where I go I'm still broken. And now I'm thousands of miles from

5

home, in a place where I can barely speak the language and I have no idea what to do.

When I return to the residence I'm going to ask Frau Wittmann for some scissors and I'm going to cut my hair. Now I have something to do. Why haven't I cut my hair yet? The old man at the next table leaves, he stops on the pavement, turns toward the window where I'm sitting and waves goodbye. He looks sweet with his little dog as they walk away. I count out enough coins to pay for breakfast. Seven euros. Seven euros is a whole lot with my travel budget. I wonder how many calls I'll be able to make with the rest of the coins. I wonder whether I'll be able to placate my mother, who's still upset over my break up and isn't going to like the idea of me being far away. Whether I'll be able to apologise to everyone at work, a job I was about to lose for arriving late almost every day for the last month. Whether I'll be able to dial the number of the place that until very recently was my home. To call Santiago after so many days without speaking and tell him: *I'm calling from Germany, how are you?* And to be focused on one thing only, one thing I ask of myself, one prayer to all the gods: that my voice won't break.

### III

When I return to the residence after walking all day it's eight o'clock and already dark. Frau Wittmann opens the door, she tells me that there's someone in the dining hall waiting to see me. The impossible image of Santiago, the absurd idea that he's come to get me has my heart surging into my mouth.

'*Me*, you're sure?' I ask.

'It's another student from your country who wants to talk to you,' she explains without looking at me.

I smile in disappointment and thank her. Before going in I ask her for a pair of scissors and Frau Wittmann tells me she'll look out a pair. When I enter the dining hall I see a dark-haired guy sitting there, disproportionately large and rather boyish. He's bent over a book about chess. He raises his head and his face lights up when he sees me. I estimate that he's around twenty-five years old. He says he's been waiting for me all afternoon. I've never seen him in my life but he acts like we're family or lifelong friends. He tells me he's from Tucumán and that his name is Miguel Javier Sánchez. That he has a scholarship from CONICET and another from DAAD, that he's studying political economy, that he arrived a week ago and that he found out today there was another Argentinian staying in the residence. He asks me what I'm studying. I lie and say I'm doing a postgraduate course in German theatre. Frau Wittmann interrupts us, she hands me a pair of scissors and warns me to be careful with them. I thank her. Miguel Javier chatters away like people from the north are famous for. He tells me about his life back in Tucumán, about his humble origins, about how proud his family is of him, the first one to go to university, the prodigy. He asks me if I want to visit the castle with him tomorrow. I tell him sure, that it's a beautiful walk and going there is one of my happiest childhood memories. He gets excited, says he'll bring sandwiches and a camera that he bought with the first instalment of his scholarship money. His enthusiasm is kind of endearing, at one point he says: 'I've read the castle's beautiful.' The sentence is all one word, '*vreadthecastlesbeautiful*. Then I stop listening to him, he carries on talking and I think about how I'm going to cut my hair. First I'll cut the ends and then

I'll keep going up with the scissors as far as I dare. It doesn't matter if it looks bad, no one knows me here. Miguel Javier is a horrible, cacophonic name. Hearing the two names together, the way he introduces himself, is an assault on the ear. Miguel Javier asks me what I'm thinking about, says I seem distracted. I tell him that it was a long day, that I'm tired. I say goodbye and agree to meet the next morning at breakfast.

After showering and cutting my hair, I feel exhausted. I collapse onto the bed fit for an exiled princess, a fake student, a solitary tourist, a refugee. I am safe. There's nothing better in the world at this moment than being alone in my rented room, my European sanctum free of luxury but full of comfort, the sturdy shutters on the window, the white duvet, the perfect pillow. I remember the story of the princess who proved her blue blood by detecting a little pea through seven mattresses. The poor thing didn't sleep the whole night. But I'm a fake princess and nothing's going to keep me from sleeping. I begin to fall asleep without troubling voices, without shaking, without worries, and I feel triumphant: I came to Germany to sleep soundly. I smell the clean sheets, I imagine that I'm another person, someone who only cares about what they're going to do tomorrow, what they'll have for breakfast, what streets they'll explore.

I'm awoken by knocking on my door. For a few seconds I think I dreamed it, but the knock comes again and I see that it's light outside. I get up and open the door in my nightdress. The guy from Tucumán is standing in front of me with an expression somewhere between cheerful and disapproving: '...'seightthirty!' he says.

I ask him to wait for me downstairs and give me a minute to change. I close the door and I get dressed murmuring words I should've said: *What's that face for? Never knock on my door at this time again, you tactless Tucumano.*

I go down to the dining hall, the scene is the same as the day before, except now among the students there's someone I know. There he is, standing in line for the coffee maker; he waves a spoon when he sees me come down and calls: 'Over here! Here!'

Once we're sitting at the table the Tucumano explains that the coffee and milk are supplied by the residence but that the students buy their own food, label it, and store it in the fridge. Since I don't have anything to eat for breakfast he shares his food with me and warns me that the shops are closed on Sundays so I'd better buy my groceries today when we return from our outing. Among the things he offers me are ham, cream cheese, and quince jelly. Then he shows me a Tupperware container full of sandwiches oozing with mayonnaise and tells me that he made them this morning, really early while I was still asleep.

The castle is located in the highest part of Heidelberg and the walk from the residence takes an hour. The Tucumano strides ahead with his camera and every ten steps he turns around to tell me something or take a picture of me. He looks at my image on the camera's screen and criticises my haircut, saying that I looked much better with long hair. We don't know each other well enough for him to make comments like that, I think, but the landscape is beautiful and absorbs any annoyance my companion might provoke. Halfway through the walk I feel tired and need to stop. Miguel Javier makes fun of me. A family of Americans who were several yards behind us catch up, and ask us to take their picture. It's a fortysomething couple with three kids who range between about five and twelve years old. They pose for the picture like models. When I return the camera, the littlest kid hugs me. The mother pulls him away by one arm and they keep walking. I remember my dream from the night I arrived, the boy's tiny hand that kept slipping away as we fled from the farmer who stared at my tits. The Tucumano looks at me and says I'm pale. He opens his backpack, takes out the Tupperware container and offers me a sandwich. I tell him I don't want one, that I don't feel well, and I vomit at the side of the path. The Tucumano holds my forehead and when I stop vomiting he gives me water and a paper napkin to wipe my face. We sit for a while, in silence. From up here we can see the river cutting through the city, the red roofs, the Baroque towers. I tell the Tucumano that I feel better and I stand up to continue walking.

'I think you're in the family way.'

'In the *what*?' I ask, stunned.

'Pregnant,' he answers, and he doesn't talk to me for the rest of the way there.

The tour of the castle costs ten euros which we pay grudgingly. At the entrance they tell us to wait for the Spanish-speaking guide, that the tour will start in ten minutes. Miguel Javier doesn't look at me or talk to me, it's like he doesn't know me from any of the other tourists in the group. I break the silence.

'How would you know?'

'What?'

'How would you know... how would you be able to tell that I might be pregnant?'

The Tucumano looks at me with a new expression; his face, which I'd considered boyish, now suddenly seems mature, as if it holds within it some ancestral wisdom.

'I have six sisters and almost twenty nieces and nephews. I witnessed all their pregnancies and all the symptoms down to the strangest things you can imagine. I know what it's all about. There's the vomiting, and to top it off you have that look in your eyes.'

'What look?'

'That, like, shiny look, like a drunk person.'

'You don't know me, maybe I always look like that.'

'Maybe, but if I were you I'd take a test and let the father know.'

The guide shows up and asks us all to gather around so we can start the tour.

## IV

I wait three days before taking a pregnancy test. I make stupid calculations: if July has thirty-one days and August does too, my last period must have been... I don't remember. I don't remember hardly anything about the last month of my relationship, just flashes of fights, cutting insults, the light turned out, Santiago's body on top of me, no eye contact, sadness. I don't remember the date of my last period. On the other hand, I do remember the night I went to Leonardo's house and we drank too much vodka and I told him I was going through a break up and he asked me to stay the night with him, and I remember my body on top of him in his bed, his snoring in the early morning and my urge to escape to some place that was mine, a place of my own, far away from everything.

I rack my memory for spots of blood, sanitary towels, Ibuprofen but I don't know what month these images belong to. It angers me to have to relive the things I came all this way to be rid of. I might still get my period. I've been sleeping more than ever lately, missing breakfast, going out for walks around midday and coming back to take a nap. One day I start talking to a Japanese girl from the residence, she's nice, she studies German, her name is Shanice. She is pretty much the only person I speak to. I realise her stay here is also an escape, but a better organised one. For a Japanese student, a semester in Germany is like a holiday. Shanice, like most students in the residence, is several years younger than me. One afternoon she tells me how she decided to leave Japan after two of her university class committed suicide. Smiling, she says: 'Throwing yourself onto the tracks is easy, so easy you could do it even if you're happy.'

Miguel Javier gets up really early and spends all day on campus so we hardly ever cross paths. I wait three days and on the third day I'm still late. I don't know how to ask for a pregnancy test in German. I ask Shanice to help me. She listens attentively and treats it as a secret mission that she has to carry out to perfection.

A little while later she's in my bedroom holding out a box she bought at the pharmacy. We read the instructions in three languages: pee in the little cup, place the little stick inside, wait three minutes, if only one line appears it's negative, if two appear, it's positive. Okay, that's simple. I thank Shanice but she doesn't leave. She stands there looking at me, waiting for me to go into the bathroom and announce the results. I gather my courage and ask her to leave me alone. She tells me no, that she's not going to leave me alone at a time like this. She stands firm like a Japanese soldier and I feel indebted to her and too tired to explain anything. I take the test into the bathroom. I follow all the instructions: I pee in the little cup, I set it on the floor and put the little stick in it. I wait the three minutes it says on the box. I try to distract myself by looking in the mirror. My face is more and more like my mother's every day. She was pregnant with me when they arrived in this city and didn't know it. Did they celebrate when they found out? Did my dad go out to buy bread, sausages, a bottle of wine? Did they toast?

Did they stay up all night making plans, call their families right away to give them the news? Did they laugh?

I squat down to get a closer look at what I just saw standing up. Two bold, well defined lines. I turn the stick over, I shake it, I look at it again and the two lines are still there. I wash my hands and leave the bathroom. Shanice is sitting on the edge of my bed and she looks up expectantly. I tell her the truth: 'It's positive, I have to think about what I'm going to do.' And I make two urgent requests: 'Please go and please don't tell anyone.' Shanice hugs me before leaving me alone. I lock the door behind her and pace across the room a few times. Then I sit on the bed. I open a packet of cookies and an apple juice that I bought that afternoon. The juice is delicious and I feel all my muscles give way, my chest feels hollow and my jaw trembles. I bury my head in the pillow and sob until I fall asleep.

# TWO

## I

It's raining in Heidelberg. It's Saturday and the dining hall has become a meeting place for the students who've had their weekend outings ruined. After an entire day without leaving my room I decide to go downstairs. Miguel Javier is playing chess with a bearded redhead. I've seen him before, I think he's from some Eastern European country and they're classmates at the university. I'm happy to see the Tucumano after so many days and I sit at the table next to theirs waiting for them to finish playing so I can talk to someone for a little while and shake off this feeling of being shut up. The Tucumano gives me a sidelong glance while remaining focused on the game. He moves one of his knights.

'Do you feel better?'

'Yes, I'm fine. You were right.'

'Of course I was, I'm always right.'

The redhead makes a move I don't see and the Tucumano gets irritated. He puts his hand on his forehead and mutters insults between his teeth. The redhead looks at me and smiles.

I think my presence distracted the Tucumano and it's my fault he's losing now. I get up and move to an empty table beside the window where I can look at the rain-soaked garden. Frau Wittmann comes over and asks me to help her hang some curtains that just came back from the cleaners. I assume she chose me because I'm alone and I'm not doing anything. Everyone else in the room is talking or reading or holding Skype calls in different languages. How is it that the manager of such a large residence doesn't have anyone to help her? She hands me the curtains, yards of heavy fabric that I have to hook to the rods over the window. I stand on a table and Frau Wittmann gives me instructions from below. Seeing me standing there the Tucumano gets up and tells me to get off the table, says I'm irresponsible. Since our walk to the castle, since my tell-tale vomiting on the side of the road, the Tucumano hasn't stopped treating me with a certain disdain. All his initial enthusiasm has turned to disappointment and he's hardly looked at me or spoken to me except to say two or three things with a disapproving tone. Now he's quit his game of chess and is standing on the table following Frau Wittmann's orders. I silently obeyed him and got down, and now I'm standing on the floor unsure what to do. I want to help but don't know how. I really don't know what I'm doing in this place, in this residence where I don't belong, in this conservative storybook city, in this repulsively perfect country. I go to my room to put on a jacket and go out. I walk in the rain rehearsing words, phrases, tones of voice. I look for a phone to call Buenos Aires.

I insert two one-euro coins and dial my old phone number. As it rings I pray that no one answers, I know it's a mistake to call with so many uncertainties but I can't make myself hang up. I resolve to be very direct, to just spit it out. It all boils down to two things, the only two things I know for certain: I'm in Germany and I'm pregnant. Ten thousand kilometres away, Santiago answers the phone. I ask him how he is. He tells me that Ringo was hit by a car and is going to have an operation. The news makes my stomach turn. I start crying again. I ask him what the vet said, if he's going to be all right. He says he doesn't know and that's life. I think about how Ringo is the single living thing Santiago loves most yet he uses that same old sarcastic tone, the same one he used when we broke up. He tells me that if I want to be there for the operation it's going to happen tomorrow morning. I tell him I can't, that I'm in Mar del Plata. I don't know why I lie, it's the first thing that comes to mind. He remains silent for a minute and then asks me to send him our Telecentro account number so he can change the bill over to his name and have them stop charging the service to my card since I don't live there anymore and it's his responsibility to pay the phone bill. 'Yep, I'll send you an e-mail,' I answer. We both fall silent again. He asks me if I have anything else to say. I tell him I don't. He says we should hang up then, that the call from Mar del Plata is going to be expensive and that he has to give Ringo his medicine. 'I hope he's all right,' I say. 'I hope you have fun in Mar del Plata,' he answers and hangs up. I freeze for a moment with the phone in my hand. When I hang up the receiver, the phone returns a one-euro coin and three ten-cent pieces.

I walk slowly, still hearing Santiago's voice in my head, squeezing my fists inside my jacket pockets. I can't imagine Ringo in pain, the very idea makes me feel nauseated. In Heidelberg there are no stray dogs rummaging in the trash or lying in the shade like in any neighbourhood of Buenos Aires. The dogs here are all purebred, small, and walk on leashes or carried in their owners' arms. There are restaurants that don't allow children, but do allow dogs. I wander for a little while longer. Now the rain has become a melancholic drizzle. I don't want to spend money in some café but I also don't want to keep getting wet. I start heading back to the residence and I think of Ringo, his warm furry body, remembering how comforting it felt to hug him when I got home in winter, his eyes, which looked at me as if he understood everything, his ears that moved up and down depending on our moods, his way of lying in the patio to nap in summer, how he stuck his nose in everyone's backside when they came to visit and how he wagged his tail every time he heard Santiago's keys in the door. I miss him and I know I'll never feel the same about another dog again.

## II

When I get back to the residence Shanice greets me wearing a fuchsia wig and a striped dress. She says she was looking for me, that it's karaoke night. In the little while I was out they've decorated the dining hall for a party, with balloons on the walls and a mirror ball hanging from the ceiling. Shanice tells me that she wants me to be on her team. I tell her that my singing is terrible and that I want to change out of my wet clothes. She gives me a blue wig and a purple feather boa and tells me she'll be waiting. It'll be fun, we're going to dress up and forget our problems, she assures me in a high-pitched squeal as she waves her hands in excitement.

My options for tonight are: go to bed, replaying the

unpleasant phone conversation over and over in my head, calculate the dates, again, to determine the percentage of likelihood between Leonardo and Santiago, then cry till I fall asleep, or participate in karaoke night. I choose the latter. I take a hot shower and go down to the dining hall. I'm wearing a dress, the only one I brought, and the purple boa. I carry the blue wig in my hand. Everyone is dressed up and happy. A German rock group I've never heard of is playing. Shanice grabs me by the arm and drags me to a corner, she puts the wig on my head, straightens it, and tells me it looks gorgeous. A boy in a ski mask and a pipe asks me to dance, introducing himself as Subcomandante Marcos. He speaks with an accent that at first sounds Russian. He dances very badly but it's funny. He asks me what I'm dressed as.

'I'm an outer-space princess.'

'Must be a character from your country.'

'Yeah.'

'If I were you I would've dressed as Evita.'

'How do you know I'm from Argentina?'

'I've been watching you since you got here.'

'Oh. Are you some kind of Zapatista spy?'

'No, I'm an Albanian womaniser.'

I suddenly recognise him, it's the bearded redhead who was playing chess with the Tucumano this afternoon. The music stops. Shanice, visibly drunk, grabs the microphone and asks for silence so she can say a few words. I've never seen her so excited, her über-perfect German now a confusing mish-mash of tongues.

'Good evening everyone! Welcome! Karaoke night, hooray, viva karaoke! Viva music! Today we all sing and dance and no one sad. Many prizes. A kiss for the winner! Hmmmm who will it be? Maybe you, the guy in the bunny costume, who will kiss you? The girl in the bunny suit, of course! Yeah, it's a party and everything goes, okay? No one sad. Viva Heidelberg! Let's see what the first song is…' she takes a little piece of paper out of a bag and reads it. 'It's: 'Papa Don't Preach,' the old hit by Madonna. Who's coming up?'

A Mexican guy wearing a gold robe and a Marilyn Monroe wig goes up to the front and does an absurd imitation of Madonna. Next up is a French girl dressed as Little Red Riding Hood who sings a Britney Spears song and then the Tucumano goes up, dressed as a gaucho, to sing "Matador" by the Fabulosos Cadillacs, with some Chinese guys pronouncing the lyrics phonetically as backup singers. It's all very funny and even though I had to force myself to participate, I have to admit that Shanice was right: for a while I manage to forget about the horrible conversation with Santiago, my pregnancy, my terrifying uncertainty. Also, there are delicious sausages and really good beer.

The fake Subcomandante Marcos asks me to go outside to smoke a cigarette with him. The night has cleared up completely and the moon is enormous like in some romantic comedy or in a werewolf movie. We talk a while about our countries, about politics, about what we like and don't like about Germany. He tells me that he's learned about Peronism in his political science courses, that he'd love to visit Patagonia, and that he's a fan of Maradona. Marcos, I still don't know his real name, takes off the ski mask and smiles at me. His smile gradually becomes a seductive stare as he passes his gaze slowly over my forehead, my mouth, my neck. I know that at any minute he's going to try to kiss me. I can tell he's very young, like the Tucumano, he can't be over twenty-five or twenty-six years old. He moves close to me and brushes aside the fringe of the wig, he says my eyes shine in the moonlight or something to that effect that I don't fully understand. I tell him that I'm probably ten years older than him and that I'm pregnant. He looks sceptical for a second but immediately realises that it's the truth. 'I'm fascinated by pregnant women,' he says as he presses me against the wall and kisses me on the mouth. For a moment something inside me resists, but quickly my arms relax and my mouth opens. I like what he's doing. I bury my fingers in his terracotta beard, we kiss. His hair is red and feels like straw. With my hands now on his head an image makes me stop cold, it's the terracotta-coloured rug that Santiago and I bought in Salta that looked so nice in front of the couch. Red and straw-like, a rug that looked rustic but was very expensive and was a worthless lie in the end, because playing house is a game that can be abandoned for any other game at any time. Something suddenly became clear to me: I don't want to buy a set of coffee mugs ever again, or straighten pictures on the wall, or decide where to put the rug that looks rustic but isn't. I don't want to go to the plant shop and ask which ones like sun and which are houseplants. I don't want to choose the fabric for the curtains, or the colour of the bedspread, or the size of the bookcase. Those rugs that everyone brings back from the North prove that it's all a lie. I'd rather live like a refugee forever, sleeping in other people's beds, having coffee out of strange mugs, mugs that I didn't choose and that I don't care about because I don't even remember the name of the street of the house I woke up in. I'd rather be surprised when I open the window, wonder whether it's a nice neighbourhood, what it would be like to live there walking on rugs with no history, or with other people's history because everything is always the same anyway. The redhead stops kissing me and looks at me in silence. I apologise, tell him I was distracted because I remembered something. He slowly moves back toward me, rests his whole body against mine and runs his hands up and down my arms. An irrational urge moves up from my feet all the way to the roots of my hair. I hug him desperately. He unhooks my bra through my clothes with one hand, lowers the strap of my dress and kisses my shoulder. I'm embarrassed by the thought that someone might see us, I pull up my bra strap, I smile at him. He grabs me by the waist, as we kiss he slowly lifts my dress and I feel his hand move up my legs until he hooks his fingers into my knickers. I think I hear someone calling my name from inside. As if by reflex I push him away and straighten my clothes, he says something in his language that I don't understand. Then he takes a step back, lights a cigarette and looks at the street silently smoking. I try to talk to him but I can't think of anything to say and once again we're two strangers, uncomfortable, outside a party.

I hear the Tucumano calling my name over the microphone: 'I want the other Argentinian to come sing a *chacarera* with me!' And he shouts my name several times. I don't know if I feel sorry or embarrassed for him and I realise he'll only stop shouting if I go inside. I tell the redhead I'll be right back. The Tucumano is lying on the floor with the microphone in his hand, some people are laughing at him while others are trying to help him up but he just repeats: 'The other Argentinian, I want the other Argentinian to come. The other Argentinian who's knocked up.' I take the microphone from him and tell him he's an idiot. He stands up and wobbles as he tries to talk to me.

'Be careful with that Yugoslav guy. *Hesathirdrate-gypsywanker.*'

'I think you're drunk.'

'*Ithinkyourebeautiful.*'

He falls back to the floor. I bring him a glass of water but he's passed out. Shanice is swaying barefoot alone in the centre of the dance floor, not paying attention to anything else that is going on. One of the Chinese guys helps me move the Tucumano to a couch where he lies down muttering insults at us. Some of the students have started clearing the tables. It's not late but the party seems to be over. In the back I see the fake Subcomandante Marcos sitting next to the French Little Red Riding Hood who sang the Britney Spears song, they're looking into each other's eyes and I can see his hand rubbing her leg insistently. It's annoying and funny at the same time. I look around the room, they're experiencing what they'll remember in the future as the best time of their lives, their student years, their foreign adventure far away from their parents. In ten years they'll probably be exhausted, they'll have kids, good jobs, and they'll look back fondly on these days in Heidelberg, days they'll never get back. But I don't belong to this group. Even if I crossed the whole world looking for a place to feel at home, I wouldn't belong anywhere. 'It was a nice party,' I tell Shanice, who doesn't seem to hear me. And I go to bed without saying goodnight to anyone.

### III

Monday very early someone slips a note under my door. Since it's written in Spanish I know right away it's from the Tucumano. It says:

*Forgive me for the scene on Saturday. I hardly remember anything, too much alcohol. Yesterday I slept all day. I wanted to tell you that I'll go with you to the doctor. You have to see a doctor. I asked around and the university hospital has good gynaecologists. I'll be waiting for you downstairs at breakfast, I have the pretzels you like. And then we'll go to the doctor.*

*Miguel Javier*


Do pregnant women have to go to the doctor as soon as they find out they're pregnant? Is that necessary? I feel fine. I hardly get nauseous anymore and everything feels pretty normal. I think the Tucumano is overreacting but deep down I'm happy that someone's worrying about me.

When we enter the hospital the Tucumano walks confidently to the information desk, makes an appointment and quickly finds out where we have to wait and which examination room we'll be in. There are three couples waiting to see the doctor before us. I find the whole situation extremely uncomfortable but I resist the urge to flee. The Tucumano smiles sympathetically and asks me if I want him to get me some coffee. I tell him no, and then I start explaining things, as if I'd already given it a lot of thought:

'Look. Miguel, I still don't know what I'm going to do. I'm outside my country and in less than two weeks I'll be out of money. Another problem is that I'm not sure who the father is. It might be my ex, but it could also be another person. So because of all that and because right now, at this exact moment, I wasn't expecting it and because I'm not sure about anything, maybe – I still haven't decided – but maybe the best solution would be to have an abortion.'

'*Yourecrazy.*'

'No. I need you to help me say all that to the doctor. We're in Europe, they're not going to be shocked.'

The Tucumano sits quietly, looking noticeably upset until they call us in to see the doctor.

The doctor is a man of around sixty, dressed in his

white coat. He bears some resemblance to Barenboim, the pianist. He asks my age, my weight, if I've been pregnant before and if I've had any illnesses. When I tell him it's my first pregnancy he wants to know why I waited so long to have kids and I realise I won't be able to ask about an abortion. I also realise that he took it for granted from the start that the Tucumano is my husband. He tells me to lie down on an examination table behind a screen and to get undressed from the waist down. I silently obey. As he touches me with his latex gloves I look at the ceiling and try to think of something else, I want to sing a song in my head but I can't remember any, so I sing the Argentinian national anthem. I sing it silently two times all the way through and just when I'm starting the third round, at 'see noble equality enthroned' I feel him pat me on the knee to signal that he's done. He takes off his gloves and tells me I can put on my clothes, that he'll wait with my husband on the other side to talk about the pregnancy. I'm halfway through tying my shoes when he starts a kind of monologue that neither the Tucumano nor I interrupt at any point:

'Everything looks very good. The pregnancy is about six weeks along. I recommend you don't drink alcohol and definitely don't smoke. If you're a smoker and it's hard for you to quit, the hospital has free programmes that can help. The same if you do any drugs, you should stop right now. You should take folic acid for the first two months but you can maintain your regular lifestyle. Try to eat a healthy diet, rich in vegetables and fibre and avoid excessive intake of sugar and salt. I'll write you a prescription for some drops that will help with any nausea. According to my calculations the little one is due the second week of March next year. You should book an appointment to see me again in ten days. We'll do the first ultrasound and you can hear your baby's heartbeat.

Congratulations, it's a very important moment in the life of a couple, you've stopped being individuals to become a family.'

The Tucumano invites me to lunch at the university cafeteria. He has class in forty minutes but he's too worried about me now. We stopped by the pharmacy to get the drops the doctor prescribed, now we're sitting at a table by the window. We order steamed vegetables, an omelette and mineral water, which according to the Tucumano are the healthiest items on the menu and good for me in my condition. We hardly speak through the whole meal. Then, in an attempt to distract myself from my thoughts, I ask him about his classes, how he's doing, if he's learning a lot, if he misses Tucumán. He tells me he misses his mum's *empanadas* and his sister Marta Paula, who out of his six sisters is the one who spent the most time with him. I think what bad taste in names his parents had. *Martapaula*, all together like he says it, is as horrible as Miguel Javier. He tells me that Marta Paula is thirty years old and has three kids. That she and her kids live with his parents because she's divorced and works as a receptionist in a hotel called Miami, near the San Miguel de Tucumán bus station. That her ex-husband is an alcoholic and that he doesn't give her any money, so he used to help his sister with some of her expenses but since he came to Germany he hasn't been able to send her anything. He misses his nieces and nephews too. Before coming here he was teaching the oldest one, who looks just like him, to play chess and he picked it up right away. Miguel Javier chose to study economics in order to understand why poverty exists, to get a clear-eyed, in-depth understanding of the situation he'd experienced all his life, and which before him his parents and before them his grandparents had lived through. It's time for his class but he doesn't seem to want to go, he's more interested in talking about his family and his studies. I tell him not to miss class, that it would be silly, then he pays the bill, says goodbye with a kiss on the cheek, and leaves. I stay to finish the coffee we've just ordered and soak up the rays of sun coming through the window. From outside the Tucumano turns and waves his hand. The light hits him and he squints his eyes, I wave with one hand as I hold the coffee cup in the other. The air smells like coffee, the sky is blue, the sun warms my face and for an instant I feel at peace, as if everything were in its place, as if everything were in perfect order.

I look at the tables, the floor, the door. I didn't tell the Tucumano but I recognised this place as soon as we walked in. I used to eat here with my mum while we waited for my dad to finish his class. The memory is so vivid that it makes me tremble. We would sit here and my mum would tell me about Buenos Aires, about the old house on the corner of Entre Ríos and 15 de Noviembre where my grandparents were waiting for us and sometimes her face would be very serious and she'd quickly turn her gaze to the window and order me to finish the food on my plate so I wouldn't see her crying. I don't know if she cried because she missed home, or just the opposite, if she was sad because we'd be going back soon and the house on Entre Ríos street was really ugly, with mildew everywhere and dust and grease that seemed impossible to get rid of and that was the house we were going to stay in until we found a place and that made her sad. Later, always, she'd remember our time in Germany as one of the happiest periods of her life. A happy exile, an exile you don't want to return from, isn't exile. But nevertheless she returned to Buenos Aires like someone going back home and she'd never set foot in Heidelberg again, and neither had I until now, after thirty years have passed and I'm older than she'd been when she looked out of these same windows.

And what should I do? Return to Buenos Aires, end my impulsive vacation, get my job back, look for a cheap apartment and have the baby? Whose baby? Mine, of course. Grey clouds pass in front of the sun. I put on my jacket and rummage for some coins to leave on the table. No, I'm not going to go back yet, not yet, I think and I sigh with relief.

## IV

A group of students, an ambulance, two police officers, and several neighbours block the entrance to the residence. The first thing I think of is a robbery but I immediately reject the idea. As I get closer I see some faces, eyes wide, expressions of shock. The redhead comes out of the crowd and he tells me to sit down, saying that since I'm pregnant the news might be too much to handle. I tell him he can go ahead and tell me, that I'm fine standing. 'The Japanese girl committed suicide,' he says, looking me in the eyes. 'What Japanese girl?' I ask as if I didn't already know he was talking about Shanice, as if I hadn't imagined this outcome a thousand times talking to her, as if I had some hope that it might be someone else, some other student I didn't know. The redhead hugs me, says he saw me with her a lot of times and that he's sorry. Then we join the group and I catch some random phrases: *they found her hanging; she left two notes; they had to notify her parents.* A police officer tells me I can't go inside until they finish investigating I don't know what. Two other men question Frau Wittmann, who clutches her head and covers her mouth with her hands. The students' reactions can be classified as either cynical or hysterical. The cynics discuss what a cliché it is for the Japanese girl to commit suicide, the hysterical ones are intermittently overcome with loud attacks of sobbing. The redhead now hugs an American girl who's crying and moaning. I turn and walk away from the scene. I want to go to the river, get some air and be alone, but a man wearing a grey suit catches up with me before I get to the corner. He wants to ask me some questions.

We walk back down the middle of the street, they've blocked the door and set up a kind of police office in the residence dining hall. We sit at the same table where I had breakfast with Shanice a few times. The man in the grey suit takes out his badge and shows it to me. I don't understand what it says but it doesn't matter. I feel a powerful and unfamiliar sense of sadness and I want the questions to be over quickly. He starts the interview, he asks me my name, my age, if I'm married, my occupation in Argentina and what I'm doing here. As I hesitate on the last question the man in the suit reminds me that this is a student residence. I tell him I'm going to enrol in a postgrad program this week. He seems to accept my answer and asks me what kind of relationship I had with Shanice. He doesn't call her by her name but says 'Miss Takahashi.' I tell him that I met her a few days after I arrived and that we hung out several times.

'How would you classify your conversations with her?'

'Classify them? I don't know, right here for example we had breakfast some mornings. She always seemed happy, she smiled a lot.'

'Did she ever mention any problems or talk about suicide?'

'No. Yes. Well, she told me that two of her classmates in Tokyo had committed suicide, but she didn't talk about any of her problems.'

'Miss Takahashi left two notes: one for her parents and one for you.'

'For me?'

'Yes. Does that surprise you?'

'Yes.'

'I'm going to release the note to you.'

The man in the suit takes out a plastic bag which contains an envelope with my name written on it. He slowly pushes it across the table to me. I open the envelope, inside is a piece of white paper with a few words written in black ink. The man in the grey suit asks me to read the note aloud.

*I had a lot of fun and I forgot my sadness for a while. Everything in my room is for you. I leave you with a hug that lasts forever.*

*Shanice*

The man says that they'll make an inventory of Shanice's belongings and that her room will remain closed until her parents arrive. Then he thanks me for answering his questions and tells me I'm free to go.

I'm upset and my heart is racing. I wish the Tucumano would get back from class soon, so I can tell him what's happened. I need to talk to someone, I need to process this and try to understand it. I feel like I'm on some kind of drug. The students look blurry, the room seems to expand and their voices are faraway echoes. I sit in the doorway until it gets dark. If I hadn't left so early this morning maybe I could've talked to Shanice, maybe if I'd had breakfast with her she wouldn't have done it. But this morning is the distant past. The doctor who looked like Barenboim now resides alongside my faded memories: my mother crying in the university cafeteria, my last night with Santiago, the karaoke party Shanice threw. I feel like this exact instant marks a break in time, as if an earthquake has split the Earth in two, everything familiar moves away forever and what's left is an endless wasteland. I'm dizzy. I put my head between my knees, I heard somewhere that it helps with vertigo. I realise I'm crying when I see tears drip from my face and splash against the floor. Someone puts a hand on my back, when I lift my head I see the Tucumano sitting beside me. I heard about everything, he says, and he offers me a blue handkerchief, very clean, which he takes out of a pocket of his jacket.

## V

Tonight my room feels bigger. The image of Shanice sitting on the edge of the bed waiting for me to take the pregnancy test is so vivid that I turn over and stare at the wall as I try to fall asleep. Her body will spend the night at the morgue. I'm consoled by the thought that the morgues here are clean places, always set to the perfect temperature. In such a charming city as this one not even places like that are unpleasant. I try to think of something else, something warm, I can't think of anything. I'm afraid it's going to be a long night. I feel around on the floor next to the bed for one of the books I brought. Packing my suitcase in Buenos Aires, I randomly grabbed a few books I'd never read. I turn on the lamp, the book is *January* by Sara Gallardo. It tells the story of a poor country girl. She's sixteen years old and she's pregnant. A disgrace. She wishes that the baby belonged to El Negro, the man she's in love with. But it belongs to another man. I think of Marta Paula, that is, I think about what the Tucumano told me about his sister Marta Paula. I imagine she's working the nightshift behind the Hotel Miami reception desk and I wonder how she'll get home; if she'll take a bus, if the bus will drop her off near her house, if her kids will still be asleep when she gets home or if they'll be drinking *mate cocido* ready to go to school. I feel very tired. I look around the room again, it seems huge and it looks different. There are pictures on the wall I've never seen before, stuck up with Sellotape: Brad Pitt, Einstein, Hello Kitty.

I pull them down and the tape pulls off strips of paint with it. I don't know when someone came in and put them up. But, of course, this can't be my room: the door is on the other side and the bed is too. Someone in the corner with their back to me rummages through a huge suitcase. It's Shanice. She laughs as she pulls out T-shirts and blouses, skirts and trousers. I'm scared but I'm also happy to see her. She's happy as always. She asks me to help her organise her clothes, that it's all for me. She shows me the tags on each shirt and dress, clothes she bought in Tokyo, New York, Paris, Frankfurt. I've never had such nice things. I think about how if I stay pregnant none of these clothes will fit and I'm disappointed. Shanice takes a long fuchsia scarf out of the suitcase. She starts to wrap it around my neck and tells me that it looks gorgeous. She repeatedly says that I have to keep warm because the German autumn will be starting soon. The scarf is tight and hot and suffocating. My arms hang limply. She notices that I can't breathe and tries to remove the scarf but she can't, her hands are very cold and her fingers are thin and stiff. She says she's going to ask Frau Wittmann for her scissors, not to worry, that she'll use them to cut the wool and get it off me. I get upset, Shanice is dead and no one will give a dead girl scissors. I wake up feeling anxious, the lamp is on. I can't stay in bed.

I get up, dress quickly and go down to the dining hall with the Sara Gallardo book. It's three in the morning. I read until the sun comes up. When I get back to my room it's already been daylight for a while.


I wake up at midday, Frau Wittmann intercepts me on the stairs and tells me in a worried tone that I have three days left to provide proof of my course enrolment. I quickly make up an excuse and assure her that I'll get hold of it soon. Then she says that Shanice's parents will be arriving this afternoon and that they want to talk to me.

I go out and have a coffee in Marktplatz, the same place where I had breakfast the day I arrived. That morning I didn't know about my pregnancy and I hadn't met Shanice yet. My hair was down to my waist, heavy as a funeral veil. That day I worried I wouldn't be able to talk to anyone but the language sprouted up from some dormant part of my brain and now I can talk to everyone. I'm meeting Shanice's parents this afternoon. What do you say to two people who've just lost a child? The thought makes shivers run up my spine. I have no idea who Shanice really was or why she wanted to leave her things to me. We had a few conversations, she laughed a lot, but that was it. And the incident with the pregnancy test was short because I asked her to leave right after. Yesterday the Tucumano said something I found comical: *the Japanese are mysterious, you can't try to understand them.* I pay for my coffee and walk along the bank of the Neckar. Some Italian tourists ask me to take a picture. When I return their camera they ask me where I'm from. For a second, I can't remember.

# THREE

## I

The Takahashis greet me with a handshake and sad but kind expressions. We sit in the residence lobby, on the sofas where some of the students made out on karaoke night. Frau Wittmann brings us tea and leaves us alone. The Takahashis ask me questions about Shanice's last days; they don't seem interested in finding an explanation for her death but rather in keeping some images of her in their memory. We speak in English, theirs smooth and fluent, mine nervous and halting, thinking too much about every word, the conjugation of every verb. I speak very carefully. But there isn't much to say. I go over each of my encounters with Shanice and I embellish them with details I think they'll like. Long stretches of silence fall between us. We exchange sad smiles and change topics for a few seconds, talking about the weather in Germany, their journey from Tokyo, Shanice's childhood in which she never wanted for anything ever. Mrs Takahashi thanks me for the time I spent with her daughter.

'She truly had great affection for you,' she says.

That's absurd, I think, any affection she had for me was unwarranted and undeserved. Shanice knew me so little that any feelings of closeness were an invention of her imagination. But I don't dare tell her parents that our acquaintance never became a fully formed friendship and I surprise myself by acting like the loss is almost as painful for me as for them. As the conversation goes on, I begin to make out Shanice's features in their faces and I start to feel like I really miss her, like I want to see her, like her absence hurts me too in some deep way.

There won't be a wake and they've decided to bury her here in Heidelberg. For some strange reason they think that their daughter had been truly happy in this city where she committed suicide, and that she would have wanted to be laid to rest here. Mrs Takahashi asks me to help her choose a dress to bury her daughter in. Then she tells me that she and her husband are aware of the note and are going to honour Shanice's wishes.

'Once we set aside the dress, the rest of the things are for you,' says Mr Takahashi.

'And for your little one on the way,' says his wife. Then, tilting her head, she adds, 'Shanice left us a long letter. In it, she told us how she'd helped you with the pregnancy test and said that afternoon she'd felt useful and she was happy, that it had been a great day.'


A few students, two lecturers, Frau Wittmann, the Takahashis, and I attend the burial. It's a leaden grey morning, the ceremony is melancholy and perfect. It could be the ending to a very sad film. The Tucumano comes running up and stands beside me. I feel like the scene has suddenly changed, that he's introduced some dissonant, strident element into it. I couldn't find any black shoes, he says in my ear. I see that he's dressed in a dark suit and wears light brown moccasins. His attempt to fit with protocol makes me want to laugh but I manage to contain it. Now Mr Takahashi cries and says some words in Japanese. We don't know what he's saying but we all understand that the sound coming from his mouth is a howl of grief. I squeeze the Tucumano's hand tightly. A suffocating silence falls over us all. Some lower their heads and fix their gaze on Shanice's grave, their eyes staring intently at the freshly churned soil as if the mystery of life were buried there.

## II

Although I try to hide my shock, the amount of stuff in Shanice's room is stupefying. Her mother holds up objects and names them. The task seems to give her some relief and for brief moments I think it even entertains her. I tell her shyly that I don't need all these things. She quickly interrupts me, shakes her arms like Shanice did and tells me that I can't refuse, that it's already been decided, that the stuff is all mine, if I don't want it it'll go straight into the trash. The Takahashis are rich, I think. Anyone could tell just by looking. In Shanice's room there are: two cameras, a mobile phone, a laptop, an iPod, an iPad, an e-book reader, a portable DVD player, a hair dryer, a makeup case, a jewellery box containing earrings, bracelets, barrettes, and necklaces, five pairs of shoes, three pairs of sandals, three pairs of sneakers, five pairs of jeans, two pairs of linen trousers, two wool sweaters, two waterproof jackets, eight blouses, eleven T-shirts, seven dresses, six sweaters, three notebooks, an electric razor, a Hello Kitty doll, a German-Japanese dictionary, reading glasses, sunglasses, a collection of postcards of castles, a map of Heidelberg, a map of Frankfurt, a book of German grammar, a book of Spanish grammar, fashion magazines, two purses, a bag, two suitcases.

When she finishes her inventory Mrs Takahashi is exhausted but her face has changed, she looks younger and more animated. We've put everything in boxes and now I'm supposed to take it all to my room. She says that she's going to her hotel to rest a while and that she'll come back later to take me out for tea. I don't know how to thank her for this huge gift, I feel strange, a bit uncomfortable. Mrs Takahashi smiles and tells me to give away whatever I don't want to keep and she leaves with short, hurried steps. I knock on the Tucumano's door to ask him to help me carry the boxes. He has a book in one hand and a pencil in his mouth, he's still wearing his suit but he's now barefoot. He tells me to wait, that he'll be right there. A few minutes later he comes out of his room with his hair wet and combed back, he's put on sneakers and he looks happy. He runs down the hallway ahead of me like a little kid going after the presents left by Santa Claus while everyone was sleeping.

Miguel Javier is more excited than I am about the stuff I inherited. As we empty the boxes in my room he shouts out phrases such as: *No way! That Jap had a lotta cash!* I give him a scolding look, he apologises but then he says it makes him angry when rich people commit suicide, that he respects it but it makes him angry. I open the box of shoes and realise they're all too small for me. I ask the Tucumano what size shoe Marta Paula wears. He tells me that he doesn't remember but that he's sure Shanice's shoes will fit her and we decide to make a parcel to send to Tucumán.

We fill up a box with the shoes and some of the clothes. Then we look through Shanice's camera and phone. There are videos she made of herself cleaning her room, taking notes in class, buying shoes, walking up to the castle. In some she speaks Japanese, in others German, describing everything with an exaggerated enthusiasm. I don't know if she was planning to send these videos to someone or if she simply liked to film herself. Most of them are boring and silly, but the video of the castle is different, it's beautiful. Shanice goes up in the cable car, there are shots of several smiling tourists and then a view of the city below while she sings a Japanese song. It sounds childish but sad and she sings beautifully. I remember my walk up to the castle with the Tucumano and his prediction of my pregnancy, I also remember the times I went up in my childhood, they're fuzzy, happy memories but they're tinged with a melancholy. I wonder whether the day she made this video Shanice had already decided to kill herself. I watch her going into one of the castle courtyards, she films her shoes, very pretty blue ones that we've just put in the box for Marta Paula. Those shoes will soon walk the worn carpets of the Hotel Miami, the floor of Miguel Javier's old house, the streets of their neighbourhood, which is called 'Palmeras'. I read the address that the Tucumano writes on the box. Hotel Miami, Palm Trees neighbourhood. I wonder if Miguel Javier realises how ridiculous these place names are. Shanice films a ruined wall covered in ivy. The shot is very long, it lasts seventeen minutes, never moving from the wall. The Tucumano repeats: 'the Japanese are mysterious, you can't try to understand them.'

As promised, Mrs Takahashi comes back to get me a few hours later for tea. She's changed her clothes, and is now wearing a light-coloured dress, very different from the dark heavy suit she'd worn to the burial. I'm tired and would prefer to stay in and nap but I accept the invitation. We walk to Marktplatz, I show her the place where I had breakfast the day I arrived, I tell her about that first day, my long walk past the places from my childhood that I only barely remember now. Mrs Takahashi is interested in everything I tell her and she shows it by opening her almond eyes very wide and smiling at everything she thinks is nice. She interrupts me briefly to make comments on how beautiful the city is and how grateful she is to be somewhere new. She points to something on each corner and thinks everything is fantastic. Her attitude would be perfectly normal to someone who didn't know she'd come here to bury her only daughter this morning. When we're about to enter the café she asks me if we can go somewhere with more young people. I don't understand her question and I have to ask her to repeat it several times. When I finally under- stand I offer to take her to the university cafeteria, which is full of students. She smiles widely and waves her arms exclaiming: 'yes, yes, I want to go there!' We take off in that direction.

Mrs Takahashi is fascinated by the place. She orders herbal tea and pear cake for the two of us. We are surrounded by twentysomething students from all over the world. Some of them might've been Shanice's class- mates. Mrs Takahashi watches them with the teacup in her hand.

'I'm turning sixty-two this year, can you believe it?' she says.

She really looks much younger. Her face has almost no lines and her eyes have a sparkle that seems excited and expectant. I don't know what to say, I talk about tea, about the cake, about the delicious German pastries. She now stares at a black student, possibly Central American. She looks at him in a way that begins to make me uncomfortable and she tells me that he's beautiful. I smile, nodding my head and I understand that, at least as far as she's concerned, we've become friends and that things are going to keep getting stranger.

'Do you think that the foreign students have more sex than the Germans?' she asks.

I remember the Albanian and our fleeting encounter. 'I don't know, I haven't really noticed anything like that,' I answer.

Mrs Takahashi tells me that when she was pregnant with Shanice she felt sexual desires towards all men, it didn't matter if they were ugly, or even if they were related to her. Mrs Takahashi laughs loudly. Then she lowers her voice and tells me she was always faithful to her husband and that she regrets it, that life is too short and sex is the best experience we can have. The black student is drinking coffee at the table across from ours with a group of young people who laugh and swap lecture notes, and from time to time he looks up and gives us brief glances. I wonder what Mr Takahashi is doing, if he's able to get any rest, if he's closed the blinds of his hotel room to be in the dark, if he's crying. I tell Mrs Takahashi about Shanice's videos, I ask her if she wants them, if she wants me to make her copies. I tell her that there's a pretty video of her going up to the castle. She says that Shanice used to send her those videos and that she doesn't need me to make her any copies. The black student stands up and leaves with his classmates. Mrs Takahashi follows him with her gaze and he turns his head for a second to look at her. She sighs, takes a sip of tea, and after a while she tells me that she wants to extend her stay in Heidelberg for a few weeks, that her husband has to return to his affairs in Tokyo but that she's decided to stay. 'What are you doing tomorrow?' she asks me. I try to make something up but I can't think of a good excuse.

'Nothing special,' I tell her.

'I want to visit that castle,' she says and then asks me to please show her the way. We agree that she'll come by the residence for me in the morning.

### III

My room is full of Shanice's things, spread out across the floor and on the bed. I still don't know how much it's all worth but I'm glad to have a laptop again. I think I'll sell one of the two cameras, the money could pay for the next month's rent at the residence. I open Shanice's computer, hundreds of documents pop up before my eyes, almost all of them in Japanese. There's a folder of photos from her childhood, her father beside her in many of them. A beautiful and chubby-cheeked little Japanese girl posing at an amusement park, inside an ice cream parlour, a train station. Mr Takahashi, twenty years younger, is very handsome. What about his wife? Shanice's mother doesn't appear in any of the images.

I should copy all these folders and clean out the hard drive before I start using it. With a new computer I could at least connect to Buenos Aires. I'd like to stay up a little longer but I'm overcome with exhaustion. Maybe it's because of the pregnancy, I think. I fall asleep murmuring things I don't understand.

It's raining. Mrs Takahashi hasn't come. I finish breakfast in the dining hall and decide to go back to sleep. I remember Shanice's computer, I was up till three in the morning last night sorting through her things. The activity silenced the nagging voice in my head that constantly asks: what are you going to do?

I assume Mrs Takahashi has cancelled the outing because of the rain. Now that I have a laptop and I can get on the internet I should answer my e-mails. The very idea puts me in a bad mood. Back in Buenos Aires it was something I did every day, but here it's different, here the time passes in a strange way and nothing is the same. How much longer will I be able to disappear from the internet too, from the lives of others? How much longer will the e-mails continue to pile up, their demands for explanations, their concern over things that I can't even remember anymore? How much longer will I be able to put off going home? And what if everyone forgets me? A forgotten person is like a dead person, and no one wants a dead person to show up in the world of the living. Before I know it Frau Wittmann is sitting at my table asking me for my proof of enrolment. Her voice shakes me out of my daze. I tell her that I'll have it by this afternoon. I put on one of Shanice's raincoats and walk towards the university in search of a solution.

## IV

A tall blonde secretary greets me at the student services office. I explain that I'd like to enrol in a postgraduate seminar, preferably something related to literature or history or anything in the humanities. I know that my request is pretty absurd, that this is not the way things are done. The secretary stares at me for a moment, silent and impassive. I know that given my poor German my request must seem odd, and she's trying to figure me out.

She shows me applications, forms, academic timetables. She tries to be friendly but she's resolute: the semester has already started and course offerings are closed for enrolment. I want to ask her if maybe there's some kind of workshop, something extracurricular, but she's already gone back to her work and isn't looking at me. I feel dizzy. I go out in search of water and somewhere to sit. There's a class in session next to the office I just left. The door is open so I go in and take one of the last empty seats. No one notices my presence. It's a huge semi-circular room with wood panelling. I think I remember this place, the smell, I have the impression that I've been here before. The professor has a familiar accent. He speaks very good German but his *R*s and the cadence of his sentences sound Argentinian. I ask the girl sitting in front of me what this course is called. 'Latin American Ideologies,' she tells me. And something that could only be classified as a miracle occurs. I recognise the professor. It's Mario, my father's old student who lived for a while at our house here in Heidelberg. He'd fled Argentina after they raided his house and he was here learning the language and finishing his degree. We'd go for ice cream in Marktplatz and I taught him to order the flavours in German. I went up to the castle with him several times and he always made up a new story to tell me on the way. There was one I liked a lot, I don't remember it now, but I know it was about a princess named Whiteflower who'd baked a cake in the castle's kitchen and the cake had grown and grown until it reached the ceiling and kept growing till it broke through the roof. That man standing there lecturing on some theory or other of Astrada is Mario, the nervous boy who bit his nails, who cried when he received letters from Buenos Aires, who whistled while he washed the dishes, who taught me how to peel an orange in a spiral. This awkward, slightly past-his-prime man, with thick glasses and a gravelly voice that everyone is listening to attentively, was my first friend.

Mario wipes his glasses, puts them back on, looks at me again. I've just emerged from the crowd of students who are asking about exam dates and reading lists, said *Hola Mario*, and his face turned red. I imagine no one here calls him by his first name and that very few speak to him in Spanish. He smiles shyly, searching his memory, murmurs words and half-phrases. I think there's no way he'll recognise me after thirty years. Mario hugs me. Now I'm the one turning red, I can't believe he remembers me. We laugh, we hug again. Some students come up, they call him Herr Professor and they talk about an article they have to read for the next class. He asks me to wait for him, says he can't get over seeing me here, that it's the nicest surprise he's had in years.

Mario invites me to his house. On the way he admits he only recognised me because I look so much like my mother and because a while back he looked me up on the internet and saw some photos of me. He lives alone in a fairly large apartment that he's been renting for many years. We make some spaghetti with sauce and we don't stop talking for a second. I tell him everything: I talk about my pregnancy, about how I'm not sure who the father is, about Shanice's suicide, my Tucumán friend, Mrs Takahashi, my life in the student residence and the growing pressure from Frau Wittmann. Mario listens with an understanding that puts me at ease. After lunch he goes to find some boxes and starts to show me photos and letters from our old life in Heidelberg. In the pictures I'm a little girl and he's several years younger than I am now. He tells me about how he was able to adapt and how he decided never to return to Buenos Aires although he should've gone back on several occasions. He says he wouldn't be able to bear walking those streets now, that his first and greatest love disappeared in '79 and his parents are dead. I understand now that Mario is gay, that he always has been. The great love he's talking about was a beautiful boy with large eyes and a happy face, he shows me several photos of him. He says that he couldn't bear to be in Buenos Aires without being able to see him, having to imagine everything they did to him, that he isn't brave enough to face it, like the families of the disappeared have, that he'd just go crazy with sadness. He says all this with barely any emotion, as if he were explaining some natural phenomenon.

He offers to go and talk to Frau Wittmann, show up in person and assure her, as a university department head, that I'm a student. I tell him that any kind of paperwork he could get me would be enough. He asks me what's so special about living there. I don't know how to explain it, being there is like not being anywhere, it's being alone but surrounded by a lot of people, having everything without owning anything, and being able to pass unnoticed. I say that it's cheap. He offers to let me stay at his house, he says there's a spare room and that I can stay as long as I want, and I thank him and tell him that I'll keep it in mind. He insists that as the pregnancy advances it would be better for me not to be alone. Outside it's still raining. Old and yellowed photographs lie on the white tablecloth alongside the breadcrumbs, plates stained with sauce and empty glasses. We both fall silent for a moment then we clear the table, carefully putting away each photo like some treasure we alone know the value of. We make coffee. Mario promises that he'll take care of the enrolment certificate today and we smile at each other, both feeling a little less alone and a little stronger.

# V

It's dark when Mrs Takahashi finally shows up at the residence. I'm about to shower and get into bed when I see her standing in the doorway wearing a black dress and bright red lipstick. I tell her that it's past the residence's curfew and I'm not allowed to let her in. She asks me to come out. She says she has a taxi waiting, that she wants to take me to dinner. I tell her that I plan to have a bowl of soup and go to sleep but she pleads with me, begs me to join her. We get in the taxi. I ask her about Mr Takahashi, she tells me that he left that morning for Tokyo.

'Where do the students go at night?' she asks me anxiously.

'I don't know,' I tell her without trying to hide my annoyance.

She puts the same question to the taxi driver who drops us off at a dark and noisy bar where they serve a lot of alcohol and not much food. I promise myself that this is the last time I agree to something like this. But for now I'm already here so I try to make the best of it. I look at the menu, there's a drink special that comes with fries and other appetisers. I ask the waiter to make the drink with very little alcohol, repeating myself several times because the music is really loud. Mrs Takahashi orders champagne and fish croquettes. Two Germans of indeterminate age come over to our table and ask if they can join us. Mrs Takahashi says yes. The waiter brings us our food and the Germans order beer.

'What are you doing here?' one of them asks.

'Girls' night out,' Mrs Takahashi responds.

'*Oh, gut, gut, gut,*' says the other and he asks us why we're in Heidelberg.

'We're tourists,' I answer but Mrs Takahashi raises a hand to interrupt me.

'I came to bury my daughter who was a student.'

The Germans look surprised and they ask her to repeat herself, saying that there's too much noise and they couldn't hear her. She repeats herself, raising her voice: 'I came to bury my daughter who committed suicide three days ago, but that's done with, now it's girls' night out.'

The Germans exchange a worried glance. The waiter brings them their beers. Mrs Takahashi proposes a toast to this beautiful city full of beautiful people. The four of us raise our glasses, we toast and drink in silence. Then, one of the Germans, the taller one, tells us that he's celebrating the first anniversary of his divorce and that he's happy to be with such pretty ladies. Mrs Takahashi laughs. I begin to feel dizzy. Mrs Takahashi gets up and starts dancing next to the table, she looks radiant. The taller German now does the same, trying to dance with her. The other one looks at me and says I look pale. I want to get up but I can't. I tell him that I feel bad and I vomit on his shoes. The German screams and I vomit again. The waiter comes over and insults us; Mrs Takahashi tells everyone that I'm pregnant. I ask her to call a taxi to take me back to the residence right away. In a patronizing tone, the taller German explains that pregnant women shouldn't drink alcohol. Mrs Takahashi hands several banknotes to the waiter, goes outside, and stops a taxi.

We're silent for most of the ride until she says gravely: 'Shanice admired her father and she was afraid of me. She was afraid of turning into someone like me, but she was always just like me. There was no escaping it. She was brave, don't you think?'

I say that I don't know, that we both need rest, that it's been a difficult few days. The taxi stops in front of the residence, the cool air when I get out is refreshing. I turn and wave to Mrs Takahashi before going in, from inside the car she nods her head slightly and I think she might be crying. I go inside before the taxi drives away.

# FOUR

## I

In the morning the world is spinning. I have to sit on the bed for a minute until I recover my balance. My body is adjusting to a lot of changes and I have to be patient with it. I feel bloated and I'm tired all the time. The brief outing yesterday with Mrs Takahashi was exhausting. Today, after sleeping all night, my eyelids are still heavy and I have cramps in my arms and legs. I'd like to spend the morning sleeping but I told Mario I'd meet him after his class. I look through Shanice's things for something to wear, all my clothes are dirty. I put on a pink shirt with hearts on it and a skirt that's too short for me. In Buenos Aires I would never wear something like this. Here, I can wear whatever and I'm too tired to keep trying on clothes. On the way out I greet Frau Wittmann, who's reading the paper. She lifts her gaze and gives me a smile: 'New look,' she says and goes back to her paper.

I arrive early, the class isn't over yet. I sit in one of

the seats near the door. Mario translates aloud from a work by Carlos Astrada. I catch some of the words but it's hard for me to make sense of them. When he finishes the text, he repeats the last paragraph. Slowly and clearly he reads: Man must always confront the immensity of earthly uncertainty – human evolution, the paths towards self-fulfilment – he must foster the relationship between the temporal plane of existence and the self, the two fusing in the heart of the self, the only constant in the process of human history.

Then he closes the book and says goodbye to everyone till next week. I greet him and once again we're amazed to see each other and we hug briefly in the middle of the lecture hall full of tall students heading out for lunch.

We eat in a fancy restaurant Mario only goes to on special occasions. He says that we have to talk, that he was thinking about me, that he thinks it's crazy that I'm here wandering Heidelberg with no plan, no job, no contact with Buenos Aires, avoiding the situation with my ex, and so on and so on.

I turn my food over with my fork as I listen to him. Shanice's clothes are kind of tight. I want to go back to my room, put on my nightdress, and sleep the rest of the day. Mario now pauses his long speech and looks at me expecting an answer. I ask him if he has a washing machine at his house. He says he does and of course I can use it whenever I want. And we both fall silent for a long while. Now I should say something to reassure him that everything is fine, that I'm just taking some time, that I'll go back to Buenos Aires and everything will fall into place. I search for the right words and try to convince myself they're true, I try to appear calm, show him that despite the circumstances I have everything under control.

'Why did you come to Heidelberg?' he asks me

before I can open my mouth.

I smile. 'I don't know, maybe all my life I've idealised my childhood here, maybe I remembered this city as a place where time passed in a different way. Here, we hoped that everything would get better so that we could go back, and in the meantime, we were in limbo, far away, happy.'

Mario stares at me silently, and I understand that those same years meant something very different to him. The words he read today in his class are stuck in my head like a catchy song: 'the immensity of earthly uncertainty', 'the temporal plane of existence'. I repeat them solemnly, as if Astrada's words might somehow explain my directionless wandering, the parenthesis I've opened in my life, this suspension of time that's hard for any responsible adult to understand. Mario laughs and tells me to come back to his house whenever I want. He likes the idea that something he said got me thinking, even in a vague way, and his concern for me seems to evaporate as we order dessert and plan trips to Frankfurt, Mainz, and Berlin.

'Autumn is coming,' he says when we leave the restaurant. 'Do you have some warm clothes?'

'I have everything, Mario. I have everything.'

## II

I take Shanice's laptop down to the dining hall. I've decided to log in to my e-mail and face whatever's in there. I didn't want to do it in the solitude of my room, for some reason I feel safer surrounded by people. I open my inbox and everyone is there: family, friends, bosses, co-workers, people I don't know, notices from the bank, overdue bills, ads. All waiting for a reply, and me on the outside looking in at them with no answers. I'm exhausted by it and I'm about to close the computer when one name jumps out at me from the long list of menacing subject lines. From: Marta Paula Sánchez, Subject: Thanks for the shoes. I open it, it's a short message that immediately relieves my guilt over not opening any of the others. Marta Paula writes that she received the package her brother sent and she wants to thank me. She also says that she'd like to thank the original owner of the shoes, but she knows that unfortunately she can't. Miguel Javier told her about Shanice's suicide and that the Japanese girl had more clothes than all of his sisters put together. She asks me if I know what made her do such a thing, what terrible thoughts she must have had. She tells me that she talked to her co-workers at the hotel and that one of them thinks it must've been unrequited love, but that she doesn't think so. She closes by asking me, when I get the chance, to please write back to her. That she can get online at the hotel where she works, and that when she works the night shift she has lots of time because there are hardly any guests to take care of, that she's going to be anxiously awaiting my message.

Responding to Marta Paula is a breeze. My fingers would feel so heavy writing any other e-mail but now I hit the keys with the speed of a typist, as if a frenetic voice inside me were dictating the sentences. I tell her I don't know why Shanice committed suicide, that I don't think there's any explanation, that her mother thinks she did it because she didn't want to turn out like her but that it's all a mystery. I write that today I wore some of Shanice's clothes, but that soon hardly any of them will fit me because I'm pregnant. That in the past I'd wanted to have kids, but that now I don't. That a while back I'd wanted to get pregnant and I'd persuaded my boyfriend, my ex-boyfriend that is, and we'd tried for two years but we couldn't make it work. And then I don't know what happened, we started to fight a lot, things got worse and worse and I stopped wanting to have kids. That one night we had a really bad fight, I don't even remember what it was about, and he told me that he was glad we didn't have kids, that I'd be a terrible mother and he also said other things that were so horrible I felt like his soul was rotten. That I left our house and wandered the streets and I remembered that I'd been invited to a birthday party by a guy named Leonardo who worked at the real estate agency we'd used to rent our apartment. That day I'd run into him on the subway and out of nowhere he invited me to his birthday. And that night I went to his party after fighting with my boyfriend, and he was happy to see me there alone and I stayed till after everyone else had left, and we started drinking the vodka he got as a gift, and I stayed all night and that maybe I was pregnant with his child, that it's very likely but I'm not sure. I tell her that I saw a doctor and it seems like everything's going fine, that he asked me why I'd waited so long to have kids and I should've said that I'd tried before but not now, that now just thinking about it makes my whole body tremble, that sometimes it all seems like a joke, a cruel joke that nonetheless makes me laugh, that I'm afraid I'm going to go crazy because all of a sudden I'll start to feel euphoric, that I'm afraid I might just stay in this city forever and never return to Buenos Aires. I apologise, tell her I don't know why I'm telling her all this, that her e-mail just asked me about Shanice's suicide and again I say that I didn't really know her well enough to be able to explain what happened, that I'd like to know too.

I send the e-mail without re-reading it. I know if I wait another second I'm going to lose my nerve. I don't know this girl and I shouldn't be telling her such personal things. I send it right away so that I don't delete it. I feel the need to tell her everything because even though she's a stranger I think of her as someone I can trust, and because now I'll be able to look forward to her response like advice from a friend.

### III

Mrs Takahashi appears in the doorway. She came to see me. She's carrying several packages. She says she was shopping all day and since she was close by she wanted to check up on me. I offer her coffee. I see that her eyes are moist and her mascara has run. I think: one cup of coffee and that's it, I'll tell her to go, find some friendly excuse to get rid of her. I bring the coffee out into the lobby and we sit in the same place we talked the first time we met. Mrs Takahashi's eyes look me up and down and I remember I'm wearing Shanice's clothes.

'They're Shanice's clothes,' I say trying to act like it's no big deal, 'I think they might be a bit tight.'

Mrs Takahashi doesn't respond. She looks at something behind me and her expression changes, like she's possessed by some strange force. I turn around. There's nothing out of the ordinary, just the dining hall and the stairway that leads to the rooms.

'Are you okay? Mrs Takahashi, are you okay?' I repeat it several times. She doesn't respond. She keeps staring at nothing, her small eyes tense and wide.

Suddenly, when I'm about to go and get help she looks at me, smiles, takes a sip of her coffee and says: 'I've never visited Buenos Aires. Do you think I should?'

I tell her that it's an interesting city, and I wonder if I

should get someone, I wonder if she might be dangerous. Now she casually opens the bags and packages one by one to show me the things she bought: an antique ashtray, a small porcelain doll, a silver watch, two dresses, a bottle of perfume.

'I'm a wandering soul in search of beauty,' she says like someone reciting a poem. And then she starts to babble in a euphoric trance: 'I've been all around town looking at young men and buying gorgeous objects, I can't complain. It's a shame the afternoon got cloudy. Is Buenos Aires very sunny? I used to hate the sun but now I love it. The sun is life and it's my time for adventures! Daughter's gone? Well fine. We mothers can also live wherever we like. Have you been to St. Mark's Basilica in Venice? It's magnificent, amazing architecture. What should I see in Buenos Aires? I want to dance tango! Daughter's gone, I can go where I want. It's our fault for giving her free rein, indulging her every whim. What beautiful clothes you're wearing! Are they from Argentina?'

'No, they're Shanice's...'

'Shanice's?'

'Yes, they're the clothes she gave me...'

Mrs Takahashi jumps in her chair as if something suddenly startled her. 'I should go,' she says without looking at me and walks hastily to the door. I shout that she's leaving her things behind but she doesn't hear me. Through the window I see her get in a taxi. Her new purchases are spread out on the table alongside the empty coffee cups.

I walk over to Frau Wittmann, who has turned on the radio. 'Mrs Takahashi forgot all these things...' Frau Wittmann smiles, something they're saying on the radio is funny to her. 'Shanice's mum forgot these things,' I repeat.

'Oh, we'll call her hotel to let her know,' Frau Wittmann says. 'What's the name of her hotel?' The radio announcer says something funny again and Frau Wittmann chuckles.

'I don't know… I don't remember the name…'

'Then we can't call. Don't worry, she'll be back to get her things.'

The idea that Mrs Takahashi might be back in a little while makes me nervous. I tell Frau Wittmann that she didn't seem well, I tell her about her absent gaze and her strange behaviour. Frau Wittmann suddenly seems interested, she's forgotten about the radio and is nodding enthusiastically as I try to explain.

'Then we'll keep her things here in the lobby and when she returns I'll give them to her myself,' she says.

I thank her and we talk a little while longer about Shanice, how quickly time passes and about autumn, which is almost here. We gather up the bags and I notice that Frau Wittmann stops to look at the porcelain doll.

'It's really beautiful,' she says. 'I had one like it in my childhood, in Hungary. Have I ever told you I was born in Hungary?'

'No, I don't think you have.'

'That was a long, long time ago.'

This is the most personal interaction I've had with the woman since I've been here. As she talks, I look at her watery blue eyes and try to calculate her age. She must be seventy or older. I imagine her childhood during the war, I notice the lines around her eyes, her thin lips, her sharp nose. For a brief instant I think I catch a glimpse of the face she had as a girl, her features round out and the colour rises up from beneath the dusty layers of suffering and joy. Once again the radio announcer says something that amuses her and I take the opportunity to say goodbye.

As I'm going up to my room I hear the phone ring. Frau Wittmann answers and begins speaking horrible Spanish: *Sí, aquí ella está.* She comes to the stairs to tell me that I have a call from Argentina.

# IV

I answer thinking it must be my mother but a strange voice says my name and then begins to explain in a slow shy tone: 'This is Marta Paula, Miguel Javier's sister, the one you sent the shoes to. The girls at the hotel and I read your e-mail, and… ya know? We thought about Feli who's a psychic here in Tucumán, she lives in La Aguadita, ya know? And… we thought of going to ask her about your baby, so you'd know who the dad is and you don't have to worry. Since I had the residence's phone number because of Miguel Javier I wanted to call you to let you know, ya know? So you don't have to worry. I'm going to go to Feli's tomorrow and then I'll call you. I'm going to hang up now because I'm calling from work and it's long distance. Hope you have a nice night and say hello to my brother for me, if he's around. Oh, don't tell him anything about Feli because he doesn't like that sort of thing. He doesn't believe in anything. Tell him I called to thank you for the package and… ya know? I have to go. We'll talk later. Bye.'

That night I dream that I go into a theatre, it's an old theatre, abandoned. Everything is covered in dust and the curtain is closed. I sit in one of the seats near the aisle and I stare at the stage, I know there's someone behind that curtain, someone waiting to make their appearance. I hear some sounds. I move in my seat and the floor creaks. Then the curtain opens, an old man dressed as a king walks across the stage. He speaks in English and I think he's reciting Shakespeare. Now the man looks me in the eye and asks if I understand. He asks me in German, and I answer in Spanish. I say that I understand. I clap. I don't

59

know what to do. The man dressed as a king asks me if I know how to act. 'I don't think so,' I answer. 'Perfect, I'll teach you,' he says. He asks me to come up on stage so we can rehearse the work he's written. I go up, he gives me a script and a crown to put on my head. The lights blind me. When I look back at the stalls I see that they're now full of people. I think I see Shanice among them. I play my part the best I can. I think about how far Shanice has travelled to get here. The man leaves me alone on stage for my final monologue. I go off script and improvise a beautiful speech. I speak first in German and then in Japanese. I close with a simulated hara-kiri, an emotional dance that ends in an explosion of prolonged applause. When the applause stops, I descend a little ladder to get off the stage and I look for the way out of the theatre.

Shanice comes over and shyly congratulates me on the performance. I thank her. Then she speaks in Spanish with a Tucumán accent:

'Ask Feli.'

'What? About my pregnancy?'

'No, ask her about my mother... so she can warn you.'

'Warn me about what?'

'Warn you that my mother is full of a very dark sadness... and, ya know, that she can get inside you.'

I abruptly wake up with a pain in my chest. I open the curtains. It's not morning yet. I go to the bathroom, drink some water, and go back to bed. I lie there trying to fall asleep. I touch my belly with both hands and I hear myself speaking in the plural for the first time, speaking not just for me but for us: *We have to sleep a little while longer but we'll try not to have any more bad dreams. We'll be all right. Tomorrow is a new day and we're going to feel better.*

# V

Mario comes by in the afternoon to take me to his friend Joseph's photography exhibition. On the way there he says: 'Joseph's work is really worth seeing. I don't usually go to this sort of thing but this is really meaningful, important work. You'll see. A lot of the artists here are bland but this guy is very talented.'

Before we go in he seems nervous, excited, and happy. Inside, he barely pauses in front of the photos, he's looking around for someone, looking anxiously for his friend Joseph who finally comes over with a glass in his hand and says: 'I've been waiting for you, I was afraid you weren't coming!'

They stare at each other for a second and I gather that they are lovers. Or they were in the past. Or they're about to be. And that Mario is hopelessly besotted. Joseph is about my age. For a moment all the other people around them cease to exist. They break their stare as Joseph moves on to greet other people. But from across the room each one will have the other's eyes stamped on his back.

Joseph doesn't have a German face. I read a brief summary of his life and work in the programme they gave me when we arrived: '*Turks in Germany' is Joseph Shoeller's first exhibition. Son of a German father and a Turkish mother, the photographer centres his work on the clash of these two cultures…*

A woman's gravelly voice calls my name from behind. What is Mrs Takahashi doing here? I greet her apprehensively. She says she went by the residence to see me and Miguel Javier told her I was here. She's wearing a black cocktail dress, but it's wrinkled, as if she hasn't slept and has been wearing it since the night before. She stands in front of one of the photos and describes it aloud: '*A*

*Turkish Family*: a father, a mother, a little boy and maybe an uncle. Look at the mother! She's Turkish! It's a Turkish mother!'

Mario seems to wake up from his amorous trance and comes to my aid, he asks me quietly who this woman is. I answer: 'it's the mother of the girl who committed suicide.' Mrs Takahashi looks at us, I was certain she didn't speak Spanish but now I have my doubts, as soon as I said 'the girl who committed suicide' she turned around. She comes toward us, she asks Mario if he speaks English, if he understands her, and she tells him that she came here to bury her daughter and has extended her stay a few more days because this city is so wonderful.

Joseph comes over and invites us to dinner. Mrs Takahashi immediately says: I know a fantastic Thai place nearby. Joseph smiles politely and says he had somewhere more modest and inexpensive in mind. Mrs Takahashi, gesturing wildly with her hands, says: 'Dear God! It's on me!' I don't have time to intervene, whether to warn Mario about my unease with Mrs Takahashi, or to make up an excuse and disappear. It doesn't seem fair to leave them alone with her. After all she came to the show looking for me. Now we're walking to the Thai restaurant. Mario seems to walk with a slight stoop and I wonder when that happened to him. In what moment did he stop being a young refugee from Argentina and transform into an ageing Herr Professor? His face however is radiant. He and Joseph walk ahead of us talking about the show and laughing like little boys. Mrs Takahashi and I follow a few steps behind. We're silent, watching the couple in front of us and I think we're both a little bit jealous, a bit envious. Mrs Takahashi suddenly breaks the silence with a sigh and says Joseph is beautiful. I answer with a weak smile, but I immediately realise that he truly is stunning. And although he has his back to me, I'm surprised to find myself imagining him naked, imagining the heat of his body next to mine, imagining our limbs entwined, rolling on the ground laughing like two teenagers in love. Joseph turns around and asks us if we're going the right way. His teeth are white as a wolf's and he has large, dark eyes with long lashes surely inherited from his Turkish mother.

'Yes,' Mrs Takahashi answers, 'We're almost there.'

## VI

Dinner passes uneventfully. Mario and Joseph keep the conversation flowing naturally. The dishes Mrs Takahashi recommends are pretty good. Maybe this life I'm living isn't so bad. I'm in Heidelberg with these three people who are, you could say, my friends. No one who saw us sitting here eating and laughing would say this is a hard life. We're about to order dessert when Mrs Takahashi gets up to go to the bathroom. The three of us are silent for a moment as we look over the options. I take the opportunity to tell them that I think Mrs Takahashi is having a nervous breakdown. They both think she's a charming woman and a very strong, dignified person. 'Yes, no, no, no, what I mean is that she's...'. Mrs Takahashi returns from the bathroom. She gives me a cold, empty stare, the same stare she gave me the previous afternoon.

I wish I could leave. Why am I here? What is this place? How can we order a dessert we can't even pronounce? For a second even Mario seems like a complete stranger, foolishly grinning nonstop at another stranger. A Turkish man with a dazzling smile, who I keep imagining naked, taking me in his beautiful brown arms.

Mrs Takahashi asks Mario where she should go to learn tango. Mario says he doesn't know. But that it should be easy to find on the internet.

Joseph stops a waiter and asks him a question about the menu.

I tell them I have to go. The three of them look confused.

'They still haven't brought dessert,' says Joseph.

'What do you have to do?' asks Mrs Takahashi.

Nothing, I can't think of anything. What could someone like me possibly have to do, someone with no responsibilities, who left home and everything behind. A useless person wandering around this unreal city. Nothing, I don't have anything to do. But I'm pregnant and that's a good excuse for anything.

'I just remembered I have a doctor's appointment tomorrow and I have to be up early.'

'Let me go with you to your appointment,' says Mario.

'No, you don't need to do that,' I tell him.

'Yes, yes I do. I'll come and get you tomorrow and I'll go with you.'

# FIVE

## I

The night before our big trip back to Buenos Aires, the night that our house on Keplerstrasse filled up with philosophers and I looked at the sky identifying constellations, Mario cried in the kitchen. I found him washing the dishes when all the guests had left and my parents were finishing packing suitcases and boxes with clothes, books, and some of the few belongings we'd cherished during those years in Germany. I stood silently watching him as the running water hid the sound of his sobs. When he saw me standing there he dried his hands and face with a tea towel, lit a cigarette and asked me if I was going to write to him when I got to Buenos Aires. Every day, I promised even though I only knew how to write my name and a few random words. We hugged each other tight. Thirty years passed between that hug and the next one. In the beginning Mario would send me postcards of castles with made up stories written on the back. I eagerly awaited those letters, which were also the first texts I learned to read. In my imagination, after our departure he'd gone to live in one of those castles and one day I would visit him and we would get married and be very happy. Now I suppose that when we moved out of the house on Keplerstrasse Mario must have gone to live in a residence like this one. What was his life like until he became Herr Professor? Did he have boyfriends? And that beautiful Turkish man, what's their relationship? Why am I scared to ask him?

He's going with me to see the doctor tomorrow. Once again I'll have to go through all that: the hospital, the anxious wait, the latex gloves, the unsolicited recommendations. I wish I didn't have to.


## II


I'm awoken by knocking at my door. It's daylight and evidently Shanice's alarm clock didn't work this morning. I open the door in my nightdress, Frau Wittmann is standing in front of me with wide eyes saying that Herr Professor has been waiting for me downstairs for a long time. I'd like to run away, jump out the window, or hide under the bed and go back to sleep. I thank Frau Wittmann, apologise for having made her come upstairs, and tell her I'll be down right away.

Mario is reading the newspaper as he waits for me in the dining hall. At the table next to his Miguel Javier is having coffee with scrambled eggs and toast spread with Nutella. My stomach turns and for the first time since I arrived I skip breakfast. I greet Mario and the Tucumano comes over to us.

'Where are you two going so early?'

'To the doctor.'

'Then I'll come with you.'

'That's not necessary, Miguel, thanks.'

'Yes, it is necessary, or did you forget that the doctor is expecting to see me too?'

The Tucumano likes contradicting me and he loves pretending he's my husband in front of the doctor. He's so enthusiastic that I give in and tell him he can come too. He wolfs down his last bite of toast, puts on his jacket and beats us to the door. When we step outside the cold air hits the three of us in the face. 'Autumn has arrived,' says Mario and we walk silently towards the hospital.

They'll only let me into the doctor's office with one other person. The decision is difficult, my two friends look at me expectantly. I think about it for a few seconds and tell them that I'm going to go alone. They nod their heads and seem to approve. I leave them there, sitting in the waiting room as the doctor checks me out in the examination room. Everything's fine.

'Want to hear your baby's heartbeat?'

'Right now?' I ask.

'Of course, now,' he answers surprised.

I'd like to tell him not now, another time would be better, because I'm distracted and I'm not going to react the way I'm supposed to. There's no way I can explain this to the doctor, and much less in German.

'Alright,' I say.

And I begin to hear some little thumping noises that sound like the beat of a song, a song that contains all the melodies in the world within it.

I'd like to keep listening to that heartbeat the rest of the day but the doctor has already gone back to his desk. On a prescription pad he writes down the names of some vitamins and says goodbye until next month.

In my brief absence Mario and Miguel Javier have been talking. I can tell because when I return it's obvious they've got comfortable with each other. Mario is telling him about his favourite cousin who was from Tucumán. Miguel Javier can't believe that Mario hasn't been back to Argentina since 1977.

'Maybe someday I'll get up the nerve,' says Mario with a sad smile. 'Until now I've never wanted to.'

The Tucumano looks at him sympathetically. I'm in a very good mood and I propose we leave the hospital and continue our morning stroll.


## III


We climb up to the Philosophers' Walk, a footpath built in the early nineteenth century that climbs two hundred metres up a hillside. From there we have a beautiful view of the city, the castle and the river. It's been a long time since I felt so happy. The autumn air is soothing. We sit on a bench beside the footpath. Mario tells us that it is named in honour of the many writers and philosophers who came to this spot for inspiration. He tells us that Goethe thought up his first ideas for *Faust* here, that this same spot inspired Hegel as he contemplated dialectics, that Schumann composed his *Symphonic Etudes* sitting on one of these benches looking at the Neckar. The Tucumano says that he'll come up here when he has to write his thesis, to see if he can think of something ingenious that will make the Germans rename the path the 'Tucumán Economist's Walk.' The joke isn't funny but Mario and I smile because everything is happy right now.

The three of us fall silent for a moment, drinking in the cool air, each thinking who knows what until Mario looks at his watch and says he has to go. He says goodbye and walks slowly back down towards the city. His body from behind, tall and gangly, looks like it's been part of this landscape forever.

The Tucumano and I are left alone. Suddenly I remember Marta Paula, our phone conversation, her promise to consult a psychic about my pregnancy, and I realise that Miguel Javier has no idea about any of this, that I still haven't told him. His sister's words echo in my memory: *Don't tell him about Feli, he doesn't believe in anything.*

'I forgot to tell you that your sister called me at the residence the other day.'

'Marta Paula? Why?'

'To thank me for the shoes.'

'Just for that?'

'Yes.'

'But she didn't say anything else?'

I can't lie to the Tucumano, my face gives me away. Also I'm dying of curiosity to hear what he knows about this Feli character.

'She told me they were going to consult with a psychic to ask about my pregnancy, about who the father might be.'

Miguel Javier looks at me very seriously. Until just a moment ago I thought it would be fun to talk about this but now I can see that the conversation isn't going to end well.

'Did she tell you the name of the psychic? Did she say Feli?'

'Yes.'

'Son of a thousand bitches. Talk about idiotic... She really said Feli?'

'Yes. What's wrong?'

'Nothing's wrong. Feli is not a good person, Feli… is a horrible woman. That's what's wrong. I'm not there and she's getting into trouble is what's wrong.'

I tell him not to worry, that his sister is a grown woman and she knows what she's doing.

'She doesn't have a clue! The next time she calls you hand me the phone and I'll set her straight! Let's go, let's go or I'm going to be late for class.'

We practically run down the hill. At the bottom Miguel Javier says goodbye without looking at me and I watch him disappear down the street leading to the university.

## IV

I wander around for a while. I don't want to be shut up inside the residence, the sky is a lead grey colour and it covers the city with a supernatural light. I think about the heartbeat I heard at the hospital, *my baby's heartbeat*, the doctor called it. Bam, bam, bam, I hear with every step I take. How is it that I'm not terrified? How have I not gone running back to Buenos Aires? I walk several blocks, everything feels tight, my bra, my shoes, and I find myself laughing, I laugh at nothing, as if I were happy, as if I were outside myself.

I come to a little square on the other side of the old bridge. Some kids are doing acrobatics on a yellow metal structure in the playground. Farther back I spot Joseph, wrapped in a dark trench coat, taking photos. When he sees me, he smiles with his wolf's teeth and puts a hand over his heart. I wasn't expecting to see him again, but when he comes over I realise how much I'd wanted to. He greets me with a hug, sits down next to me and shows me the pictures he took that afternoon: a glass skylight from below, Turkish women in the door of a shop smiling at the camera, tourists with shopping bags on the old bridge, the kids in front of us frozen in mid-air. They're beautiful, I tell him. We're sitting so close that anyone might think we're a couple. The very idea makes me nervous. If Mario saw us here, the two of us here without him… But my concern is silly, this wasn't planned. We're here, and his leg brushes my knee as I look at the photos on his camera. I can't think about anything apart from touching him. He talks about the great light he had that afternoon. I noticed it too and that's why I'd continued wandering around. But I don't say anything, I smile and look back at the images on the screen and I feel the heat of his body next to mine. Now he invites me to have coffee at his house. Did he say his house?

'It's kind of cold out here,' he says.

It's six o'clock and it's already getting dark. The kids who just now were playing on the bars walk away holding their parents' hands, wrapped in colourful puffy coats.

'Maybe another day, I should go back to the residence now.'

'Tomorrow?'

'I don't know. Maybe tomorrow.'

I give him back his camera. I zip my jacket up to my chin. Joseph asks if he can take a photo of me. I think I must look terrible but I say yes. He points the lens at me and clicks three times. Then he takes a little notebook and a pen from his pocket and writes down an address.

'Can I see the pictures?' I ask him.

He rips out the sheet he just wrote on and hands it to me.

'It's my address, you can see them tomorrow when you come round.'

71

Joseph's apartment is on the top floor above his family's shop, which sells Turkish spices. He has very little furniture: a mattress on the floor with pillows, an old couch, a desk, books piled up, an electric oven, photos spread out everywhere. The window frames a view of the old roofs of Heidelberg and the sky at this time of the afternoon is reddish. I spent all day deciding whether or not to come, I tried to distract myself by helping Frau Wittmann sort old magazines to throw away and talking to her about Shanice. After lunch I took a long bath, I washed my hair, spent a long time fixing it, put on the prettiest thing I could find.

Now Joseph is making coffee and I'm letting myself sink into the couch as if I weren't planning to get up until the next day.

'How did you meet Mario?'

I don't know why I ask him this. I don't want to talk about Mario. Not with him. I don't want to think about the relationship they have or imagine them here together, naked, dressed, or in any state.

'At the university, in my failed attempt to study philosophy,' Joseph answers as he heats water and washes some mugs. I see him as if he were moving in slow motion, as if it were a sequence of still frames I want to have branded on my memory forever.

'And you became friends there?' I say and immediately regret asking such a stupid question.

'Yes, Mario is an amazing person. Intelligent, generous, with a great sense of humour. I could spend days with him and never get bored.'

Joseph smiles, he hands me coffee in one of the mugs

he's just washed and he stares at me. His black eyes are like tunnels that I want to crawl into, pass through, and face whatever's on the other side.

'You went to the doctor yesterday?' he asks me, to break the silence.

'Yes, Mario came with me.'

Again I'm talking about Mario. I can't believe it. I'd like to forget the way I saw them smiling at each other and be able to talk about him as if it were no big deal.

Now Joseph shows me some photography books he was excited to receive this morning from New York. He sits next to me and together we turn the heavy pages, one by one. We flip past portraits of exaggeratedly expressive people, urban landscapes, interiors of public buildings. Joseph touches my face, he pushes back my hair and he kisses me on the mouth. I'm frozen, sunk into the couch, my heart races but I'm calm. Mario no longer figures in my thoughts. Joseph, still kissing me, begins taking my clothes off. Suddenly we're both naked, intertwined. My body is beautiful in his hands and I wrap myself around him, as if he's what I'd been missing all my life.

We fuck all afternoon and then we fall asleep. When we wake up it's night-time. Joseph gets up, puts on a wool sweater and looks for something to make for dinner. He fills a pot with water to make spaghetti and shows me some of the spices from his family's shop. There are dozens of little jars filled with colourful condiments. I unscrew a lid and the smell is so strong it seeps into my brain. I recognise basil, cumin, bay leaf, maybe mustard. The rest are a mystery.

Every once in a while Joseph pours me a bit of wine.

'What are you thinking about?' he asks.

'That this was the best day I've had since I got to Germany. And also that it's the first time I've had sex since I got pregnant.'

Joseph smiles but he remains silent. I don't know why I'm telling him this. It wasn't necessary. It doesn't matter. I watch him as he works in the kitchen. I want to ask him to stand still so I can determine the exact shape of his eyes, his nose, his mouth, his teeth. He puts plates on the table and he says to me:

'Mario's coming.'

'Here? When?'

'At nine.'

I get dressed as fast as I can. Joseph tells me to stay, that dinner is almost ready. I don't understand him. I don't even hear him. I ask him if the door below is open, and I pray, as I walk down the stairs, that I won't run into Mario. When I get to the street Joseph pokes his head out the window and shouts something to me in Turkish.

'*No te entiendo*,' I shout, and I get out of there as quickly as I can, virtually at a run.

# SIX

## I

I walk without thinking where I'm going and suddenly I realise I'm lost, that I don't recognise the neighbourhood, that I can't tell north from south, that I have no idea how far I am from the river. There's no one around, the shops are all closed, it's almost nine and the streets are totally empty. I search for Shanice's mobile phone in my bag. It has hundreds of numbers saved in it but I only know two people, her mother and Miguel Javier. Of course I call Miguel Javier.

The Tucumano listens to me carefully as I spell out the names of the streets I see and he gives me directions to get back to what he calls 'our house'. When I arrive he's waiting for me at the door, dressed in a jacket that's too small for him, rubbing his hands together because of the cold and before I can even say hello he tells me that we have to talk.

'Fine, Miguel, but let's go inside, it's cold.'

'Before we go inside I want to talk. There are two things that upset me in life. One I can't tell you, the other is people messing with my family. And because of you my sister's got it into her head that she has to go see Feli, and nothing good is going to come of it.'

'Who's Feli?'

'Feli! The psychic.'

'I didn't ask her to go see any psychic.'

'Yes, it was her idea. But you have to call her and get that plan out of her head.'

'Call her now? In Tucumán?'

'Yes.'

'And what do I tell her?'

'That you remembered who the father is so she doesn't need to ask the psychic. And that she should stop going into the slum to see that witch. You have no idea how dangerous that freaky old lady is, not to mention her whole family of junkies. Come on, please, call her now. Please.'

The Tucumano is so upset that I agree without asking any more questions. I feel ridiculous calling Tucumán, to talk to his sister who I don't know, to make up some kind of story. Miguel Javier dictates the number as I punch it into Shanice's mobile phone. I ask him to go away, to let me talk to her by myself. The Tucumano walks slowly to the end of the block and as he turns the corner and disappears from my view Marta Paula answers. I can hear dogs barking, a baby crying, and another noise that sounds like a football game playing on a badly tuned radio. I say hello, I ask her how she is. She's elated when she recognises my voice. She first tells me some things I can't hear, then she quiets the dogs and starts talking nonstop, as if there were too many words to explain something she herself doesn't understand.

'I was just going to call you. I was thinking about going to the phone booth because I can't talk with all the noise at my house. And you just called, and you were right on time... because, ya know? I was about to call you! And I just asked my mum to watch the kids, because ya know, there are a bunch of important things I have to tell you...'

'Oh, I wanted to talk to you because I was thinking and well, I think I already know who the father of the baby is, and so... you don't need to ask anyone.'

'I already went to see Feli.'

'Oh, you already went? What did she say? Anything about the father?'

'Not at all. Nothing about the father, no idea. But she looked at my shoes as soon as I walked in. I thought she was jealous of them because she looked so serious, but that wasn't it, it was something else, some psychic stuff. I told her about you, the pregnancy, and she starts in about the shoes. They were the blue ones you sent me, I never take them off. When I finished telling her everything she started shaking in her chair and said that the woman is bad, she's dangerous.'

'What woman?'

'I asked her that too. And then she tells me that the shoes aren't mine. Yes they are, I tell her, they were a gift. And she starts smoking and she says the shoes came from very far away. Right, I tell her, and then I tell her that first they were in Japan and then in Germany, and now I have them here and I wear them every day because I like them a lot. And she says, "The girl is dead but the mother is alive. The girl knew that the mother was dangerous." She was talking about your friend, ya know? The Japanese girl! And about her mum. "And do you know why she killed herself, Doña Feli?" I ask her. And then she looks at me and she asks about you. She says that this woman is following you, that you need to come back, that you've got yourself in a mess there. Luckily you called me so I could tell you.'

The Tucumano has returned and is making gestures with his head. I make gestures with my hand for him to let me finish the conversation. On the other side of the phone the dogs have started barking again and Marta Paula seems to be in a hurry to hang up. I ask her what else the psychic said. I should tell her not to go back, but I want her to give me more information about their meeting, to figure out how Feli knows all this.

'I need to go back where?' I ask. 'To Argentina?'

Now she doesn't seem to hear me, she's talking to a little boy, telling him to turn off the TV and she tells me she has to go.

I'm left frozen with the phone in my hand. Miguel Javier stares at me in silence. Frau Wittmann peeks out from the door, when she sees us both standing there she sighs with relief and says:

'The Argentinians! You finally showed up! That Takahashi woman is waiting for you in the lobby, she came to talk to you, but since you weren't here, I had to put up with her all evening. Come in, please!'

Frau Wittmann goes inside and waits for us to follow her. I tell the Tucumano we're leaving and as I drag him down the street, I tell him about the conversation I just had with his sister. I don't know why Mrs Takahashi has come to see us but I don't want to see her. I don't want to see her ever again.

## II

It's very late and everything around the square is closed, all except for one restaurant. The menu displayed outside is too expensive for us. I think we should go in anyway and share the cheapest dish. Miguel Javier says I'm crazy, he looks at the menu and calculates the percentage of his monthly stipend that the meal would cost. He's in a bad mood.

'Let's go in Miguel, please,' I beg him.

He must be able to tell how cold and tired I am because he suddenly seems to feel sorry for me and agrees to go inside.

A waiter in a tuxedo leads us to a table. He makes an unintelligible recommendation and leaves the menu.

'Thanks, Miguel. I know I seem crazy dragging you around town and making you come in here. Your sister got me worried. How could some old lady in Tucumán know that in a city in Germany there's an Argentinian chick being followed by a Japanese woman who's the mother of the former owner of the shoes your sister was wearing?'

As I say the words I realise that as much as the situation scares me, it also fascinates me. The Tucumano gives me a grave look from over the menu and tells me that it's because she's a witch. We find the cheapest dish, pasta with meat, which we point to on the menu for the waiter.

'We're going to share it,' Miguel Javier says to the waiter in impeccable German, then turns to me. 'My sister loves getting herself into messes like this. For over a year she's been finding any excuse to go and see that witch. It started when her drunkard of a husband took off. And Feli told her the truth, that the guy was hopeless and that their relationship was over. One night she was really sad, she said she was never going to get her life together, and she asked me to go with her to see the old lady. The place is a hellhole. There are like twenty people living there, selling drugs, women, it's a disaster area. How do you think I feel ten thousand kilometres away knowing that my sister's mixed up with those people?'

Miguel keeps talking and I listen until something suddenly distracts me. Out of the corner of my eye I see the outline of a slim body dressed in black entering the restaurant. I don't need to turn my head to know that it's Mrs Takahashi. I interrupt the Tucumano, I ask him to turn around and take a look. He does. I fix my gaze on my plate and repeat a kind of prayer to make us invisible.

Miguel says slowly: 'It's her and she's coming over. Play it cool,' he orders. 'Don't let her see that we're scared of her.'

Mrs Takahashi sits down next to me.

'Look where I had to come to find you!'

'How did you know we were here?' I ask, unable to pretend I'm pleased to see her.

'I have dinner here every night, dear. I hope I can sit with you. I'm always so alone… What luck that tonight you're here too.'

Miguel and I look at her perplexed. She runs a finger over the menu and calls the waiter. She orders the most expensive wine, and three plates of tenderloin with sauerkraut. Miguel reminds the waiter that we've ordered the pasta to share but Mrs Takahashi laughs and says: 'I'm paying tonight and you two look hungry. I don't want to hear any arguments about it.'

The three of us fall silent for a while. How could this woman do us any harm? She's so small and seems so fragile. She rummages in her purse, takes out some pills, breaks them up, and swallows them in little pieces. I try to glimpse the name of the medication but she tucks the bottle away before I can make it out. Now she smiles at us and says:

'I was waiting for you two all evening.'

'And why is that?' asks Miguel.

'Because you guys have to tell me what I should do when I travel to Argentina. I want to know everything. First I want to dance tango. I learned some steps in Japan but there I'll learn for real.'

Miguel rubs his head with his knuckles. I've seen him make this gesture before when he's nervous or confused. 'I don't know anything about tango, madam.'

The waiter brings the wine. Mrs Takahashi tries it. I wish I'd stayed with Joseph. No, I wouldn't have been able to sit through dinner with him and Mario. I don't think I can see them together again and not feel awful.

'I can't have wine,' I say.

'A little bit won't hurt,' says Mrs Takahashi, and she tells the waiter to fill my glass. The Tucumano interrupts her.

'It's better if she doesn't drink. Pour me some, please, I'm curious to see what this wine is like.' He takes a sip. 'It's very good, I'm no expert on wine, but it's very good.'

'So you don't know anything about tango, young man? What kind of Argentinian are you?'

'I don't know, I just don't like tango very much. I listen to a little bit of folk music, I don't know.'

'What should I see in Buenos Aires? I want to go as soon as possible.'

'Oh, I don't know much about that either. I think it's probably a very complicated city.'

I hear Miguel's words, his accent, I see him squirming in his chair, dutifully answering the Japanese woman's questions and I don't feel like we come from the same place at all.

'You'd have to ask her since she's the one from Buenos Aires.'

Mrs Takahashi looks at me and repeats the question like a robot. 'What should I see in Buenos Aires? I want to go as soon as possible.'

'Why? Why do you want to go to Buenos Aires? What's in Buenos Aires that could be of any interest to you, Mrs Takahashi? You should go back to Japan. Back to your husband, do you understand? Go home.'

Mrs Takahashi starts to cry and pulls a handkerchief from her purse. The Tucumano looks surprised. I'm surprised too. What I just said or maybe the tone I used was cruel. I've never talked to Mrs Takahashi that way. But tonight, at this table, I feel cornered, stuck in some strange trap. I'm not going to let myself be taken in so easily.

'Travelling to Buenos Aires was one of Shanice's dreams,' she says as she wipes her eyes, smudging her mascara.

'It might've been one of Shanice's dreams but she wasn't able to fulfil it. She stayed here. You came to say goodbye to her, to make arrangements and do what you had to do. And now you need to go home. It's not easy to lose someone. You can't mourn properly if you're running around everywhere all day. Go home. Things will be better there.'

Mrs Takahashi cries harder. Miguel looks horrified. I don't think I said anything mean. Maybe the tone was mean, maybe it was the tone.

After a small heartbroken sob Mrs Takahashi seems to pull herself together. She smiles and begins talking to us as if what I'd just said was what she'd been waiting for all evening.

'Of course, Shanice dreamed of going to Buenos Aires but something stopped her. Do you know what it was?'

Miguel Javier and I shake our heads.

'She died,' she says. 'We're all masses of chaotic little particles, little leaves blown around by the wind. You want to go to the east but the wind blows you west. You want to go north but the wind pushes you south. It's not up to us.'

The waiter comes over with the three plates of food. As he sets them on the table the Tucumano says he thinks the opposite is true, that everything, absolutely everything, depends on us, that we're victims of our own decisions. He takes a bite of meat and talks with his mouth full. He arranges his napkin on his lap and he explains to Mrs Takahashi that his entire life he's seen the direct consequences of his own actions. For example, being here now is the consequence of the long nights he spent studying at his parents' humble home. He could've slept more, or gone out dancing or done drugs like other kids, but no, he stayed in to study and got a scholarship and now he's here, he says. Shanice made a decision. It was her own doing, not destiny's.

The portions are large and even though the meat is a little underdone for my taste I devour it steadily. The secret is to smother every bite in sauerkraut so I can't see the blood, which would disgust me if I weren't so hungry.

But once I've eaten almost the entire plate a wave of feverish nausea comes over me. I smile, but it's a reflex induced by my repugnance. Mrs Takahashi is talking and the Tucumano is tapping his fork on his plate spattered with juice from the meat he just finished.

'Stop with the fork!' I say. Miguel looks embarrassed. 'Sorry, but please stop doing that.'

Mrs Takahashi says I look pale and she touches my forehead. Her hands are cold as death, her icy fingers tipped with perfect nails. I pull my head away and smooth my hair. I say I'm fine, I just want to take off my sweater because this place is too hot. The Tucumano pours me some water but when I take a sip I'm afraid I won't be able to swallow it.

'She's going to be sick again, poor thing!' says Takahashi.

'I'm not going to be sick. Let me out, I want to go to the bathroom.'


The bathroom is clean, very clean. That's the way things are in Germany, fortunately. Before going into the cubicle I look at myself in the mirror for a second: my face is swollen, I have bags under my eyes and my hair looks terrible. Did Joseph see me like this or did it just happen? I feel like I might faint. I have a bout of violent diarrhoea that seems like it will never end and I'm afraid of losing the baby. I tell myself that you can't lose a baby because of diarrhoea.

Afterwards I barely have the strength to clean myself. I hear Mrs Takahashi's heels approaching. I wish I could pull up my trousers and be done with this. But I'm too dizzy. I lean over and see her shoes under the door. I tell her to get Miguel Javier, that it's an emergency. Then I see a spot of blood in my underwear, everything goes dark and cold and I know I'm fainting because it's like I'm dying.


### III


Miguel Javier says they carried me out of the bathroom. That he doesn't know how but my trousers were on and all buttoned up. And that Mrs Takahashi wanted to come with us but he politely convinced her to go back to her hotel. I'm in my bed at the residence and Miguel is holding my hand. Frau Wittmann is standing behind him and looking worried as she holds out a glass of water. I squeeze the Tucumano's hand and I tell him about the blood. Miguel tells me not to worry, that it might be nothing. I start crying, unable to hold it in, and I collapse exhausted onto the pillow which gets wet with my tears. Frau Wittmann doesn't say anything, she just sets the glass on the night table and leaves the room. I think she's annoyed that we were speaking Spanish in front of her.

'Go to the bathroom and have a wash: we're going to the hospital.'

'Thanks, Miguel.'

We spend the whole night there. They give us a room, I'm lying fully dressed on a hospital bed and the Tucumano dozes on a couch. Every once in a while two young doctors come in to check on me, take my blood pressure, listen to my heart. They give me an ultrasound. They both insist that I'm fine and that the baby is fine too. One of them asks the Tucumano if we had sexual relations that night. Miguel is silent and I say yes, that two or three times. It seems that could have something to do with it. They tell me to take it easy for a few days, avoid sexual relations for a week and to remember to take my vitamins. But why did I get so sick? The Tucumano and Mrs Takahashi ate the same thing I did and nothing happened to them. It could be emotional, the doctors say, and they flash their professional smiles as they leave the room.

# IV

'Why don't you go back to Buenos Aires?' The Tucumano is walking fast, without looking at me, and has been repeating the same question since we left the hospital: 'Why don't you go back to Buenos Aires? You tell the Japanese woman to go back home but the one who really has to go home is you because you're pregnant and you're not studying or doing anything here. At least the Japanese lady has money and she can do whatever she wants. The person who should be taking care of your problems is the father of the child. Find him. But find him yourself. And marry him or move in with him or whatever and stop messing up other people's lives. It took me a lot of hard work to get here, why can't you leave me in peace?'

Miguel Javier starts walking faster and leaves me behind. I try to keep up with him, I say I understand his annoyance, that we're both very tired and in a bad mood. But I can't catch him, my legs feel as heavy as bags of potatoes. The Tucumano walks even faster and disappears from sight. It's cold and I want to go home, but where is home? I feel nauseated. And sad.

I wonder if Joseph is awake yet, if he's alone, and I look for the way to his house.

# V

I go into the café on the corner across from Joseph's house. I order a cup of tea and toast. Coffee would be too much after last night. I sit at one of the tables by the window, from here I can see Joseph's door and his uncle's shop. If I pay attention I might see Mario leave; if I get up the nerve I might go and ring Joseph's doorbell after that, once he's alone. I can't get distracted, just a glance at the breads and cakes on the counter would be enough to miss Mario's exit. The tea is very hot and I drink it slowly as I track all the movements on the block. A few minutes ago an old man entered the café with a ridiculous dog. They're sitting at the table across from mine. The old man smiles at me and the dog, an indefinable mix of breeds, pulls hard on his leash trying to get to me. I don't look at them but I know they're there. I feel pretty good considering the horrible night I had. The tea and toast replenish my strength. I'm annoyed that the old man is looking at me. Does he think it's strange to see a woman having breakfast alone so early in the morning? Heidelberg is a small town after all and in small towns people find it odd for women to sit alone. I bet this wouldn't happen in Frankfurt. From here I can keep an eye on everything: the street, the spice shop, his door, his window, but with the old man staring at me it's hard to focus. Fine, enough, I look the old man in the eyes, he smiles at me and I realise it's the same man from my first day, from the café in Marktplatz. Does he remember me? Can he tell I'm spying on someone? The mutt breaks free and comes over to do a little dance at my feet. He's so ugly that he's cute. The old man calls him, he does it sweetly, trying not to scold him. The dog dances like a trained monkey, it's grotesque and extraordinary. It's really funny. I give him a little piece of toast which he sniffs then ignores as he continues shaking his front feet in the air.

The old man comes over to us.

'Heel Rosie, heel!' he says and I realise it's a girl.

'It's fine, I don't mind.'

'You like animals?'

I say yes, that sometimes I do. I notice that the spice

shop has just opened. The roller shutter has been raised and if I squint I can make out a lady moving around inside, maybe it's Joseph's aunt.

'You're not from here, are you?' the old man asks. Rosie, the monstrous little dog has lain down at my feet and she shows me her white belly.

'No, I'm not from here.'

'Are you Italian?'

'No, I'm from Argentina.'

'Oh, you look Italian.'

The lady from the shop leans out the door. I try to pick out Joseph's features in her face but I can hardly see her from here.

'Come on Rosie, back to our table.'

'It's fine, she's not bothering me.'

Rosie rubs her back on my shoes. I'd like to tell the old man that I had a dog in Buenos Aires that did the same thing and now I don't even know if he's alive or dead, but I don't say anything. A van parks in front of the spice shop and blocks Joseph's door. His window above remains closed. I imagine Joseph sleeps late but I know that Mario doesn't, and if they're together they must've already woken up. The old man applauds his pet's pirouettes.

'Rosie is a good little dog. She's my only company. We don't need anyone else, do we, Rosie?'

'Do you want to come sit with me?'

A few minutes ago I'd never have imagined proposing such a thing, but he and Rosie seem like friends now and I want to spend a little while longer with them. Anyway the van is blocking my view and if they join me I can order another tea and ask the old man things about the dog: how long has he had her, what breed is she, what time do they get up in the morning, where do they like to walk?

'Oh, no, thank you young lady, we better go back home, we have a lot to do. Come on, Rosie dear. Say goodbye to the young lady.'

Rosie stands up and shakes her front paws. She looks like a deformed bird. The old man leaves some coins next to his cup and puts on his coat. 'Come on, my little doggie, let's go home. Goodbye, and have a nice day.' He smiles and nods as he passes me on their way out.

I watch them walk slowly down the street. They make their way through a group of kids on their way to school. One of them bends down to pet Rosie, who wags her tail and runs around. Then they all continue on their way. Now there are more people on the street, coming and going. The van that blocked my view starts up and once again I have the door all to myself. What is Joseph doing in there? What if he suddenly comes out and crosses the street? What do I say if he sees me? *I came to see you, Joseph, I came to see what you're like in the morning. I was at the hospital all night, and I just met an old man with an amazing dog, Joseph, you should've seen her. You know, I had a dog in Buenos Aires, sometimes we took naps together on the couch. He had deep black eyes like yours and…*

No. No. Joseph is with Mario. Mario loves him and I should be in bed resting. I should be in Buenos Aires. In a house that's mine. My house, my clothes, my language. Joseph's door opens. My heartbeat reverberates through my whole body. I realise that I'm not prepared to see Mario walk out of that house with a sleepy face or his hair wet from the shower. But it's Joseph who just stepped out onto the street. I recognise him immediately even though he's wearing a long trench coat and half his face is covered by a scarf. He's alone. He's alone? Yes, he's alone. He walks to the corner and turns toward the city centre. I pay for breakfast and leave the café. I cross the street trying to catch up with him but my feet are stiff and my body feels heavy and tired. I can only walk slowly, one step at a time, as I watch him move farther away.

# SEVEN

## I

'Sorry for calling so early.'

'What time is it?'

'Here or there?'

'Here.'

'I don't know but it's later there, five hours later I guess.'

'I slept all day.'

'What I wanted to tell you was that I think I'd better not go and see Feli anymore.'

'What happened? Did you go back?'

'Yes.'

'Why? Why did you go back? I didn't ask you to go and see Feli again.'

'I went because a friend asked me to. Another girl. Not you.'

'And what, she told you something about me?'

'Yes, a lot of things.'

'Your brother is going to kill us. What did she say?'

'Strange things.'

Frau Wittmann knocks on my door. I recognise the little tapping sound, like her knuckles were made of metal. I ask Marta Paula not to hang up and I open the door in my nightdress.

'There's a man downstairs looking for you,' she says in a disapproving tone.

A man? Miguel Javier? I lean out and see Joseph at the foot of the stairs. Joseph's here! He's flipping through some magazines in the lobby, I see his dark hands turning the pages and I feel weak at the knees.

'Marta Paula, I have to hang up now but I'll call you later.'

'Tonight?'

'Yeah, later.'

'Okay, you'll call me tonight?'

'Yes. Thanks for everything.'

'All right. You have to hang up now?'

'Yes.'

'Oh, okay. We'll talk later then.'

'Yes, bye.'

'Bye.'

## II

Frau Wittmann looks me up and down. She knows I'm pregnant. She knows it even though I haven't told her. 'I'll be down in a minute,' I tell her and I close the door. I turn the room upside down looking for something to wear. Nothing fits: Shanice's clothes have got smaller and smaller and what I brought is no good in this cold. I mix one of my skirts with one of her sweaters. I grab a jacket just in case Joseph wants to take me out. It would be better to go out. I don't want to kiss him here, with Frau Wittmann watching, with the Tucumano lurking around. I should brush my hair. I'm calmed by a memory of Santiago: it's a Sunday morning, I just woke up, he looks at me from bed and says I look good with messy hair. It's a nice memory. What is Santiago doing now? What time did Marta Paula say it was in Argentina? How many hours did I sleep? I leave my room and go downstairs. I think about what the doctors said: no sexual relations for a few days. I'll have to be firm about that, though it won't be easy. Joseph, standing there, smiles at me with his teeth, with his eyes, with his thick dark hair. He hugs me, he kisses me on the head.

He tells me: 'Mario left these for you, it's the keys to his house. He went to Frankfurt for a month and you can use his house whenever you want. He left you a note with instructions for the water heater and the stove. Let me know if you need help moving your stuff over.'

He gives me a kiss on the forehead and he turns to go.

'You're leaving already?'

'Yes, I'd love to stay with you but I have a lot of work to finish.'

I watch him go. I squeeze Mario's keys in my hands. Frau Wittmann stares. I know she wants me to go, she wants me to leave the room for a real student to use. But she doesn't say anything. It's just her face, her accusing expression. I hold her gaze. 'I'll move out tomorrow,' I tell her.

'Very good,' she says. It makes me sad. I'd thought there was more feeling between the two of us. If not, then why had she shown those gestures of affection towards me? Why had she told me about her childhood in Hungary, the war, and her life? Living with strangers for so long must've hardened her, I think. But I don't want to leave it like this. I walk over to her, I thank her for the time we've shared and I tell her that I'm going to go stay with a friend.

'That Turk?'

'How do you know he's Turkish?' Frau Wittmann smiles. Joseph has a Turkish face and that's enough.

'Turks are very dirty. You understand me? Dirty. We don't have any Turkish students here, there are none. They just want to make money here. And they're liars. Whenever they can, they bite the hand that feeds them. Those Turks. And they're violent. Very violent. I don't want to have anything to do with Turkish people. What time did you say you were leaving the room?'

'In the morning, after breakfast.'


### III


Tonight I look at my residence room with more affection because it's the last night I'll spend there. As of tomorrow I'll live in a house. And maybe Joseph will sleep beside me. I hug my pillow thinking about his shoulders.

Frau Wittmann was so horrible about him, I'm sure that's why he left so quickly. What should I do? Why do I keep thinking about him? It's not too late to keep from making the situation worse. But it's beyond my control. That night Joseph pops into my head again and again. I relive the afternoon at his house and I feel an infinite happiness. I'm crazy, how can I go and stay at Mario's? How can I accept his hospitality when I'll want Joseph to sleep there with me every night? How long will I be able to last without mentioning their relationship? I don't care, all I want is to bury myself in his arms without saying a word. I'm afraid I'll start asking questions that I'll immediately regret. I'm afraid I'll say words that don't sound like my own. We could just embrace forever, in silence. Joseph. Joseph.

Frau Wittmann knocks on the door. I open it, annoyed. Anything she has to say to me she could've said downstairs. She hands me thirty euros and says it's left over from my rent this month.

I thank her and say goodbye until tomorrow.

'Do you believe in God?' she asks me before she goes. Her question catches me off guard and I don't know how to answer. I'm afraid she'll say something else about Turkish people.

'Why?' I ask.

'You have to believe in a god, don't you think?' she says as she walks away.

I close the door and get into bed. I want to go back to thinking about Joseph but I can't now. The thirty euros remind me that I don't have much money left. I plan to sell Shanice's computer or one of her cameras. I'm sure some student will be interested.

# EIGHT

## I

Miguel Javier listens silently, every once in a while stirring his cup of coffee that must be cold by now. We're sitting at the same table where we first had breakfast together the day we went to the castle, the day that he predicted my pregnancy. I tell him that I'm already packed and that in a little while I'll hand my keys in to Frau Wittmann.

'I thought you were going to stay longer,' he says.

I explain that I can't stay here, that Mario's house isn't far and he can visit whenever he wants.

'I thought you were going to stay longer,' he repeats.

We finish breakfast in silence.

I suddenly remember that I never returned his sister's call. I'll do it later, after I move and I can talk for longer. I couldn't do it last night. Seeing Joseph and that hostile conversation with Frau Wittmann left me exhausted, despite the fact that I'd slept all day.

Miguel Javier offers to move my things for me. I set the keys on the counter without saying anything to Frau Wittmann.

'Good luck with everything,' she says without looking up from the newspaper she's reading.

When the taxi arrives almost all the students have left for the university.

'What about you, Miguel? You don't have class today?'

'No, I'm not going today.'

## II

Mario's house is beautiful. Or as the Tucumano says, 'sbeautiful. We set the bags down in the living room and explore every corner. I'm happy to be here with Miguel Javier and to be able to show him Mario's things that now feel like mine. My bathroom, my towels, my kitchen, my pots, my living room, my sofa, my bookshelves, here's my little garden, my plants, my watering can, my dead bird in the grass, repulsive, swarming with ants.

'Don't touch that.'

'I just want to get a closer look.'

'I'm going to get something to wrap it up and throw it away for you.'

The Tucumano goes into the house and comes back with a bunch of paper napkins, wraps up the bird and holds it for a moment in his hands.

'I'm going to throw it away on the street.'

'How long do you think it's been lying there dead?'

'Maybe a day, maybe just a few hours.'

I think about Shanice and about whoever found her body. I remember seeing them take her out in a black bag. The Tucumano deals with the bird issue like a professional. I go into the kitchen, put the kettle on and search the drawers for a *mate* gourd. I quickly locate an enormous one with a silver rim and an inscription that says *Souvenir of Buenos Aires*. I assume it was a gift and I wonder if Mario, every once in a while, gets visitors from Argentina. I open all the containers until I find the *yerba mate* tea and I offer Miguel the first *mate* of our stay in Germany.

'No, thanks, I don't drink it.'

'You don't?'

'No, everyone in my family drinks it, but not me, I think 'sdisgusting and it gives me heartburn.'

He goes into the bathroom to wash his hands and I remember once again that I should call Marta Paula. I bet if she were here she'd have several rounds of *mate* with me and she'd tell me about Feli and everything she said to her. I can't return the call until her brother leaves.

I lie down on the sofa. Miguel comes in, looks over the books and the CDs.

'Your friend Mario has a great library. What did he go to Frankfurt for?'

'He went to do something at the university, I suppose.'

'Want me to help you unpack your bags?'

'No, don't worry about it, I'll do it later. For now I don't need to unpack hardly anything. Half of that stuff there is Shanice's, I only came to Germany with one suitcase and a backpack and nothing else.'

'On second thoughts, I'll take some *mate*.'

Miguel sucks the straw with a disgusted look on his face. I offer him sugar and he heaps on three or four spoonfuls, making it undrinkable. We talk for a while about the house and how everything works: the coffee maker, the stove, the stereo, the TV. Then he goes silent like at breakfast. I know he's sad that I'm moving out of the residence. It would be hard for me to stay there without him too.

'Do you miss home, Miguel?'

The Tucumano sucks the straw pensively.

'Yes and no. Sometimes I think I could stay here my whole life and never go back to see anyone. But when my mum or Marta Paula calls I remember things and it makes me want to be there. Mostly because I worry they might need something, that they might have a problem. My dad is old and he never knows what's going on, that's the truth. My mum cooks all day for the family and to sell. My sisters are busy with their kids, their problems. Marta Paula's the only one who helps my parents, because she lives with them, the rest don't have time. I helped her get a job. It's a really good job but she's always been the kind of person who just floats along, you know? She fell in love and had kids right away, she didn't even get to finish high school. And then her husband turned out to be the worst of the worst. He doesn't help her with money, he doesn't see the kids. I was saving up to come here and one day three thousand pesos I had hidden went missing. I wanted to die, because you can do whatever you want to me, but to think that my sister could've stolen from me was something I couldn't handle. So I confronted her and I asked her and I realised that it wasn't her. Then I found out that her husband had come by that day. So I was left with no doubt that the guy is a scumbag.'

Now Miguel Javier sets down the *mate* and jumps up from the couch with his eyes wide.

'Did you open the suitcases?'

'No.'

I sit up and see that two of Shanice's suitcases are open and clothes have spilled out.

'You must've opened them to look for something and you don't remember,' Miguel Javier accuses me.

'No, I haven't touched them since we came in,' I respond. And we argue over it for a minute.

'Are you scared there might be ghosts?'

'No, not at all. They must've opened on their own, the zips must be broken.'

## III

It's past noon and the Tucumano is still here. He flipped through several books from the shelves then turned on the TV. He's now watching a German news programme that's announcing the winning lottery numbers. I make lunch from some sausages, tomato and cheese I found in Mario's fridge. Later on I'll have to go grocery shopping. Later, after the Tucumano leaves and after I call Marta Paula. Miguel goes into the kitchen and says he heard the doorbell, he asks if we should answer it or pretend we're not here.

'No, go and see who it is please,' I say as I pull the sausages out of the boiling water with a fork. I locate plates, cups, a table cloth. Miguel comes back in.

'It's a friend of yours,' he says.

'Did you let him in?'

'No.'

'Stay here, I'll go.'

Joseph smiles at me when I open the door. I'm going to have to cook more sausages, I think. And when I let him in, I also think that his presence makes the house perfect.

I introduce him to the Tucumano who just stares and without many questions the three of us sit at the table and have lunch.

Miguel Javier asks Joseph what he does for a living. Joseph answers that he helps in his family's shop and that he's also a photographer. I talk about Joseph's photos, repeating Mario's words like a parrot: Joseph's photography is meaningful, important work.

The Tucumano eats in silence; he's confused, it shows on his face. He's so nervous that he accidently knocks over his glass and has to surround his plate with napkins to dry the mess. When we finish eating he remains seated and doesn't help us clear the table. Joseph offers to wash the dishes. Miguel Javier follows me with his gaze without moving from his chair.

'I think I need to rest a bit,' I say.

'I'm going now,' he answers and before I can say anything he gets up, puts on his jacket and walks to the door. 'Now I understand everything,' he says through clenched teeth and he leaves.

## IV

Being with Joseph in this house, just the two of us, makes me fantasise about starting a family. I watch him drying the dishes, putting things away where they belong, making coffee. He moves confidently around the kitchen, opens the right drawers, quickly finds the tea towels, the coffee cups, the teaspoons. I wonder how many times he's been here before but try not to think too hard about that.

'I think you were kind of cruel to your friend.'

'To Miguel Javier? Why?'

'It's obvious he's in love with you.'

Joseph comes over to me, cups my face in his hands and kisses me on the mouth. Is this the moment I came for, the reason I got on a plane with no plan in mind? Because simply returning to your childhood home is not much better than having no plan at all.

I tremble thinking about everything I left behind, everything I could've done in Buenos Aires in all this time, my job, my family, Santiago. What would've happened if I'd stayed there? What would've happened if my parents had stayed here, if they'd never gone back to Argentina?

'We can't fuck,' I tell Joseph clumsily and I explain that it's doctor's orders for the next few days. He looks like he's just remembered I'm pregnant, he asks how I feel, my plans for when the baby comes.

'I don't know,' I answer. And it's true, I don't know.

Suddenly I remember the idiotic face of the guy that could be the father of my baby. Not Santiago, who looks intelligent even though he's not that smart. The other guy, Leonardo, from the real estate agency. I've been trying not to think too much about him but now his face is stamped on my brain. The face of an idiot, yes, I see it as clearly as if he were right here calling me sweetheart, doll, baby, and asking me to stay the night.

Joseph says that I'll know what to do when the time comes. It's horrible to hear when I realise that 'You'll know what to do' doesn't include him at all. And now, here, the only thing I want is for this to last, for it to last a long time; forever, if possible.

We fall into a silence interrupted intermittently by small talk, about how cold it's been the past few days, my move from the residence, his exhibition next week. I'd ask him to stay the night but he seems restless and I don't have the nerve. I tell him about the dead bird Miguel Javier and I found in the garden this morning, the way the Tucumano took care of it without batting an eyelid. When he smiles I say almost without taking a breath: 'I'd like you to stay today.'

'There's something else you have to know,' he answers.

I tense all my muscles in anticipation of what he's about to say, my legs, my hands, my heart, everything.

'Mario is sick and he went to Frankfurt for treatment.'

'Treatment? What kind of treatment? What's wrong with him?'

'It's something liver-related that they haven't been able to diagnose yet.'

'I should go to see him.'

'No, he asked me not to tell you. When he gets back we'll see how he's doing and how we can help him.'

I imagine Mario in a hospital bed and my knees weaken. Joseph hugs me, we go to the sofa and we lie there for a long time staring at the ceiling.

'I'll stay over tonight,' he says and I press myself against him.

## V

Joseph and I speak in German, he generally uses easy words and phrases when he's with me. To tell me that the night we spent together was incredible he says: 'I slept well.' Then he kisses me and gets up announcing that he's going to make coffee. Last night we didn't fuck, yet I think it was one of the most intense nights of my life. What could I compare it to? A blood transfusion, an earthquake of euphoria, something like that. Lying in bed I listen to him moving around downstairs in the kitchen, I try to remember his body in the dim light. I relive the feeling of his chest against my back, his hands lifting my hair to kiss my neck. And the sound of Shanice's mobile phone ringing nonstop. The third time it rang I got up to answer it. I was naked and I wrapped myself in a blanket and went downstairs confused, thinking about Mario. It was Marta Paula. She sounded very strange. Her voice was hoarse, she almost didn't sound like herself. I apologised for not returning her call like I'd promised. She kept saying over and over 'We have to talk, we have to talk'. She said it mechanically and every once in a while she paused to let out a kind of sob, a muffled moan that troubled me greatly.

'What's wrong?'

'I'm like this because I went back to Feli's. She did something to me, I don't know… She really upset me. She told me to talk to you… ya know? To ask if you're going to deal with that woman, the mum of the dead girl, who's a very heavy burden… and she wanted to know… what I'd done with the shoes. "Nothing, Doña Feli, I have them at home." And then she kind of laughs and she says to me, she asks if I'm going to have them on when they put me in a black bag too. "What black bag?" I ask her. "No one knows their destiny for certain but you're going to have a shitty life," she says. "What do you mean *a shitty life*?" And then she makes a face like she's tired of talking to me, but I keep asking her, and then she said that everyone sooner or later ends up in a black bag, and she told me to ask you. And she told me more things, but I can't remember now…'

'Don't go back to that place, Marta. Forget everything she said.'

'I threw the shoes away.'

'Good, I think that's a good idea.'

'What's the black bag?'

'Don't listen to her. Forget everything she said.'

Then we both went silent and I heard cumbia music in the background and people talking. I asked her where she was and she didn't answer. Then she told me that for the past few days she's had insomnia. I told her that she was going to feel better once she got some sleep. That we'd talk tomorrow.

When I got back to bed I told Joseph, summarising as best I could, who Marta Paula was and the friendship we started over the shoes, about Feli, and how ugly it had all got. He said that he thought it was a fascinating story but then he wrapped his arms and legs around me and we didn't talk about anything else.

# NINE

## I

I wake up in Mario's house and it takes me a few seconds to remember where I am. The morning light is different than it was in my room at the residence; it reminds me of my house in Buenos Aires. Joseph isn't beside me, I hear him in the kitchen. What is he doing? Why didn't he wake me up? I get out of bed and as I rummage in the suitcase for a pair of trousers and a T-shirt I'm struck by a memory: Santiago making breakfast, me looking for something to wear to work, Ringo coming and going between the two of us, wagging his tail in anticipation of his morning walk. Here, in this place I hardly know, the memory of that house is unbearable, I feel guilty for having abandoned it and certain that I'll never see it again.

Downstairs, Joseph has made coffee and is toasting bread. He says he has to leave in a bit. We speak very little. I'd like him to come back to bed with me or just leave so I can be alone. I wash the mugs we just used. Joseph moves around the house, goes into the bathroom, takes water out of the fridge, goes out into the garden to smoke. I'm impatient, why is he still here if he said he had to go?

I should call Mario, find out how he is, if he needs anything. I stop what I'm doing and ask Joseph for the phone number of the clinic where Mario's staying. 'I don't know it,' he answers. I ask for the name, something that would help me find it on the internet. Mario doesn't have a mobile phone and I have to get in touch with him somehow. But Joseph doesn't have any information; Mario doesn't want us to find him, he says. How can he be so accepting, so calm?

I tell him I want to be alone. Joseph puts out his cigarette and stares at me for a moment. 'See you later?' he asks. I say 'Yes,' and he leaves.


## II


Here by myself, the house seems huge. I spend hours rummaging through Mario's things and I find the boxes he brought out the day we were reunited. I read the letters I sent him, written in my little girl's handwriting. In some I ask him to come to visit us in Buenos Aires soon, in others I tell him that I want to visit him in Germany and live with him in the castle in Heidelberg. They all close with my signature, which hasn't changed much since then, and a drawing of a heart or a star.

Among the letters and postcards there are also some photos. I immediately remember the Kodak camera we had, the square one with the flash cube on top. Many of these photos must have been taken with that camera. I'm in several of them, at the house on Keplerstrasse, sliding down a hill, in a forest, beside a lake. In one photo, there are some strange animals peering out at the right edge of the image. I stare at the picture for a long while trying to figure out what these creatures are. They look like large goats, or miniature bison, or some unclassifiable beast. The date and a brief description of the place are written on the back of the photo. It's strange that it doesn't mention the animals at all.

I come across a black and white photo of several men on the stairs of what looks like a public building. On the back, in delicate handwriting, it says: University of La Plata, 1975. And it names each of the people pictured. There are several lecturers mixed in with a few students. My father is there, among the faculty staff, in a suit that looks too tight and a big smile. Mario is there too, at the edge with a full head of hair and thick-rimmed glasses; he can't be more than twenty-five years old.


In one of the boxes I find a handful of letters wrapped up with a blue ribbon. I carefully untie it, feeling more curiosity than guilt. It's five letters to Mario from Elvio, his dead boyfriend. I read the first one dated March of '79. Elvio writes from his imprisonment in what he calls 'the cave', and assures Mario that they'll let him out at the end of the month and that they can meet in Mexico, Spain, or Germany. The letter is cryptic, as if written in code and with entire sections redacted, but it's probably the most painful text I've ever read in my life. Through the blacked out sentences I can just decipher the words 'regret', 'hell', 'pass out'. The paper has turned yellow over the years and it looks like it has been reread and refolded many times. 'They'll let me out at the end of the month and I don't know where they're taking me but we'll find each other,' he repeats further down.

When I finish this letter I don't have the energy to read the others. I go to the kitchen to get a tea towel or something to dry my tears, and to drink some water. Going through those boxes and delving into those old photos and letters has left me tremendously thirsty.

Through the kitchen window I see the patio and the little garden. In the past day it's filled up with dried leaves. I want to have everything clean and tidy when Mario returns, I don't know when that'll be but I hope it's soon.

### III

I'd been determined not to set foot in the residence again. My last encounter with Frau Wittmann was so hostile that I had no desire to see her ever again.

But the Tucumano has just called asking me to come over immediately.

'Me and Frau Wittmann and a bunch of other people are here trying to calm Mrs Takahashi down. She keeps asking for you. We can't get her to calm down. She's beside herself.'

I beg him not to give her my new address and promise I'll be there as soon as possible.

When Miguel Javier opens the door, the scene inside is unbelievable: Mrs Takahashi is curled up on one of the dining tables blubbering phrases in Japanese interspersed with words in English. Frau Wittmann paces in front of the table threatening to call the police. A few students watch from a prudent distance, laughing nervously.

'I think she's having a breakdown,' says the Tucumano. 'She was asking for you, pacing back and forth, and then she got on the table.'

Frau Wittmann rushes over and grabs me by the shoulders. 'I don't know what to do,' she confesses, exhausted.

I can see that I have to go over and talk to the woman. Everyone is expecting me to do it. I move slowly to the end of the table where her feet are and I walk around until I reach her head. 'Mrs Takahashi...' She doesn't look at me. She's lying on her side with a lost look in her eyes and she repeats: 'I'm not leaving.'

'It's me, Mrs Takahashi.'

Mrs Takahasi looks at me, slides down off the table and sits in a chair. Her movements are so elegant that they almost make us forget the ridiculous scene she just made.

'I was desperate to see you. When I found out you didn't live here anymore I got a bit nervous. That's all. I was looking for you because I haven't known what to do with myself lately. Could you...? You know I don't want to go back to my country but my credit card isn't working anymore and my husband won't answer my calls. You were a good friend to my daughter and I'm sure you can help me. I know I've bought too many things but it's not the right moment to go back yet. My husband... my husband shouldn't have left me here alone.'

Mrs Takahashi stops speaking and covers her face with her hands. Frau Wittmann and the Tucumano stand to one side waiting for me to decide what to say or do.

'She can't stay here, I've already told her that this is a residence for students only,' Frau Wittmann's rasping voice echoes through the dining hall.

Mrs Takahashi sobs, 'My daughter was a very good student. Very good! I should move into her room for a while.'

I try to think, to find some way to help quickly and leave. But Mrs Takahashi uncovers her face and takes my hands in her cold fingers.

'Let me stay with you, at least for tonight. I can't go back to the hotel. Do it for Shanice, do it for me, I don't have anyone else.'


# IV


I did everything I could to avoid it. I tried calling Mr Takahashi from the phone at the residence, offered to contact the Japanese Embassy, and begged Frau Wittmann to make an exception and let her stay there for just one night, but nothing worked. At one point I thought of just leaving. I didn't owe anyone excuses or explanations. But a horrible feeling of guilt stopped me. Mrs Takahashi was on the brink of ruin, about to break like the dry trunk of a tree blown down in a storm, her pleading eyes fixed on me.

Now, sitting in the living room of my new house, she seems to have recovered a bit. She smiles calmly and silently nods her head at everything I say: Mrs Takahashi, should I make some tea? Mrs Takahashi, if you want to take a bath I'll bring you a clean towel. Mrs Takahashi, tomorrow we'll go to the embassy to resolve this situation, you should go home as soon as possible.

I make some tea and turn on the TV. I look for a movie or some show that will make us feel less uncomfortable, something to distract us for a little while. I stop on an old black and white movie: Audrey Hepburn and Gregory Peck stroll through the streets of Rome speaking in dubbed German. Mrs Takahashi seems interested. She raises her eyebrows as if remembering something and then sighs.

'It's a nice movie,' I say. She nods her head. It worries me that she hasn't said a word. I look at her out of the corner of my eye, she seems fascinated by the movie. I pretend to concentrate on the images as I mentally consider what I should do next. First I'll have to work out where the Japanese Embassy is, or at least a consulate, I doubt there's one in Heidelberg. The second thing will be to find someone to go with her, maybe Miguel Javier... I don't have the nerve to ask Joseph and I don't want to leave this house until Mario returns. Why hasn't Mario been in touch with me? He'd know how to sort this all out.

Mrs Takahashi sighs, she seems to be in another world. With the excuse of making more tea, I get up from the couch and go to the computer to search for the embassy address. I find it right away: Hiroshimastraße 6, Berlin. There's a consulate in Frankfurt too, maybe tomorrow morning I could go there with Mrs Takahashi and try to find Mario. Spend the day in Frankfurt, or as long as it takes. I could water the plants, lock up the house, and try to take care of this. If we leave very early we could be at the consulate as soon as it opens, then I'd explain: *This woman is in a state of shock, alone, without any money and far away from her country. Please, help her, it's your responsibility.* And then I'd search all the clinics in Frankfurt until I found Mario, there can't be that many. And when I find him I'll bring him back to his house, or stay there with him, help him with whatever he needs until we can come back.

# V

I feel Mrs Takahashi's cold hands on my head and I jump in my seat.

'You have beautiful hair,' she says. 'You should grow it down to your waist.'

'You scared me… Is the movie over?'

'Oh, yes. It's an old, old movie. I think the actors are dead now. They were so good-looking. I recognised the streets of Rome. Do you think I'll ever be able to go back there? I don't think so. The time is past now. Thanks for bringing me to your house tonight, you are very kind.'

I turn off the computer, but it's slow and it takes a few seconds for the blazing Japanese flag on the embassy webpage to disappear.

'Let's go out to eat,' I say, 'It's on me.'

The woman smiles and speaks slowly.

'I'd rather we stayed here. You have such an inviting home, and I've spent so many nights in restaurants… There's nothing like the warmth of a home, don't you agree? Oh, it's so nice here. So much nicer than I'd remembered was possible.'


Mrs Takahashi is right. It would be better to stay here and get everything ready for tomorrow. I can cook some pasta, open a bottle of wine and plan our trip to Frankfurt. If I can manage to be convincing, if I can get her to pay attention to me, she'll see that it's the best thing for her and we'll be able to relax tonight.

'Do you like pasta, Mrs Takahashi?'

'Pasta? Yes, of course. I wanted to eat it all the time when I was pregnant with Shanice.'

'It must be common with pregnant women, because I want to eat it all the time too…'

'Do you know what you're going to name your baby?'

'No, not yet. I don't even know the sex yet.'

'I think everything must be easier with a boy. You know? Shanice and I never understood each other, or worse, we understood each other too well.'

'That can't be so bad.'

Mrs Takahashi smiles bitterly and runs her long fingers over her forehead. She's striking to look at, beautiful and terrifying at the same time. I go into the kitchen and she slowly follows. As I get out the food to make dinner she watches me silently, smiling slightly, her head tilted to one side as if it were too heavy to hold up.

'I hope you have a boy, you don't deserve so much suffering.'

'Don't get upset, please, let's enjoy dinner. Tomorrow is going to be a busy day. We'll take the train at six fifteen to get to Frankfurt before eight and be at the consulate as soon as it opens. Everything will work out fine, you'll see. You'll be back home soon.'

Mrs Takahashi remains silent as I finish making the sauce, open the wine, drain the pasta.

Once we're sitting at the table I again explain the plan to get her back to Japan, trying to be as detailed and optimistic as possible. She doesn't say anything, just twirls her fork on the plate hardly taking a bite. I propose a toast, pour wine into her glass and mix mine with a splash of water. 'To the future,' I say, not very convincingly. The woman follows my lead almost automatically, takes a sip and speaks slowly and quietly.

'What were you doing the day of the incident?'

'Are you talking about the day Shanice died?'

'Yes, the day of the suicide.'

'It was a Monday. I went to the hospital early. It was my first visit to the doctor about the pregnancy. At noon I had lunch with Miguel Javier in the university cafeteria. I recognised the place, I remembered eating there with my mother when I was very little. Then I walked on my own for a long while and at around six I went back to the residence.'

'And what were you thinking about when you were walking?'

'I don't remember.'

Mrs Takahashi sighs and looks at me as if hoping I'll continue the story of that day. I don't know what else to say. I don't want to tell her about the police, the students crying hysterically, the black bag they took her daughter's body away in. The Japanese woman urges me on with her expectant gaze.

I tell her that the days before that one had been fun. I tell her about the karaoke night, how her daughter had planned the party and played the host, how she'd seemed happy, radiant, that everyone was astonished by what she did. This is what I say, but it's not true. Her suicide didn't surprise me, it made me sad because as soon as I heard, it seemed so obvious. I see her again in my memory on the night of the karaoke party and I know that what she was projecting wasn't happiness, it was anxiety, it was a horrible sadness disguised with bright colours and screeching music.

# TEN

## I

I look at the alarm clock, it's four thirty in the morning. Something, some movement inside my womb woke me up. It's the first time I've felt it. I'd like to tell someone, but there's no one beside me I can wake up to say: *I think our baby just moved for the first time*. I breathe deeply and pull the blanket over my shoulders. I wait a moment to see if it's going to move again, I turn onto my side but nothing happens. I know I won't be able to fall back asleep. The alarm's going to go off in half an hour anyway and we'll have to eat breakfast, get our stuff together and head for the train station. I sit up and turn on the light. Last night, after getting Mrs Takahashi settled on the living room sofa, I packed a rucksack with my passport, money, and some clothes in case I have to stay in Frankfurt for a few days. I check to make sure I'm not forgetting anything. I also want to call Joseph and let him know that I won't be back until I find Mario. I'm going to tell him that

I've made up my mind, I don't care what he and Mario agreed. But it isn't even daylight yet so I have to wait. I lie back down, I stare at the ceiling. I'm anxious. I wonder if Mrs Takahashi was able to sleep. I feel sorry for her. I feel sad and immensely unsettled by her expression that says: it's all going to get worse, no one is safe anywhere in the world. Sometimes her gaze makes all the muscles in my body tense up. I feel hopelessly tired but now it's time to start the day, to begin our search for a solution. Yesterday I thought that all of this was going to be easy. I was even kind of curious to see Mrs Takahashi interact with other Japanese people at the embassy and explain her situation. Now it seems like a ridiculous plan, an excessively heavy burden. Getting out of bed becomes an impossible struggle. The house is colder than normal and I wonder if the Japanese woman has turned off the heating. Maybe the living room was too warm and she decided to lower the thermostat. It's our last day together and after I leave her at the consulate she's not going to get anything else from me, that's it, I repeat to myself as I put on the warmest clothes I can find.

## II

I turn on the lights in the living room. The blankets and pillow that I handed Mrs Takahashi last night are stacked neatly on the edge of the sofa but she's nowhere to be seen. I check the bathroom, the kitchen, I go into the garden thinking I might find her out there catching flies, hugging a tree, or something of the sort. What did she do? When did she leave? Where is she? What money is she going to use to get by?

I lie on the sofa and wait a while, thinking maybe she's just gone out for a minute; but her things are gone. She's not coming back, I think, and I'm not going to Frankfurt. Not on the six fifteen train, or the eight o'clock train, or any train.

Later on I go to see Joseph. He thinks Mrs Takahashi might turn up any moment and that I have to decide what to do if that happens. I notice he doesn't look at me as he talks, he's distracted by I don't know what, he shuffles papers and throws them away, sends and receives messages on his mobile phone. He says he'd like to have lunch with me but unfortunately he's in a hurry. I don't know what it is he has to do, but I envy his busyness. I don't have anything to do at all. I have a faint memory of being rushed and stressed in Buenos Aires and I want to tell Joseph that my life wasn't always this directionless drifting, that I used to send and receive messages all the time too and I was always running late and hurrying off somewhere, and that in Buenos Aires life is much more stressful than in this tiny make-believe town. Joseph apologises as he puts on his coat and hands me mine, which I've only just taken off.

'Where are you going?' he asks at the door.

'Towards the old bridge,' I say, pretending I have something to do there.

'Then I can't walk with you,' he says. He gives me a kiss on the forehead and rushes off in the other direction.

My strolls here are aimless; I move from one point to another without any rhyme or reason. I'll say to myself: *Let's go to Marktplatz*, and when I get there I'll say to myself: *Now let's go to the cathedral*. Right now I'm walking

119

towards the old bridge, like I told Joseph, and I don't know what I'll do when I get there. If someone asked, I could say that I came to Heidelberg to walk, to sleep and walk. Sleeping and walking don't sound like much, but they're both good things.

The temperature has dropped a lot in the past few days and there aren't as many tourists on the streets. In Buenos Aires the weather must be quite warm by now, the heat and humidity ramping up as the year ends. I think about everyone, I imagine what clothes they're wearing, if the heat makes it hard for them to sleep at night. I always liked summer nights, the smell of mosquito coils, the sound of the fan, the joy of staying up until dawn. The night I slept with Leonardo, the guy from the real estate agency, the likely father of my child, it was unseasonably warm. 'There's no springtime anymore,' he said, 'this is how it is now, we go straight from winter to summer,' and he kept talking about the atrocities of climate change that our offspring will have to suffer. I can hardly remember his face, I just remember the heat and the smell of vodka, and how I embraced that strange body with a silent request: *Don't talk any more.*

Maybe the time will come when I want nothing more than to return to Buenos Aires, or maybe it will never happen. I try to imagine the feeling my parents must've had, the forced decision to stay so far from home. But I don't have anything keeping me from going back, from picking my life up right where I left off. Though the life I had before is impossible now. I stop on the bridge. I rest my elbows on the parapet and look down at the Neckar, smooth and empty in the morning light. Before I came back I imagined that this part of town would've become more developed, but no, it looks exactly like I did when I lived here. It seems like nothing ever changes much in this city that has somehow escaped the bombardments and other onslaughts of history.

I run my eyes along the banks of the Neckar until I see something so disturbing that I have to look away, turn completely around and sit down to decide if I really saw what I thought I did. Crouching on the riverbank, barefoot, Mrs Takahashi was trying to put one of her feet into the water. How can I be so sure it was her? It looked like her same straight hair, all in a mess, her same long-sleeved black dress; but she was too far away to be sure, it could've been someone else, it could've been anything.

### III

I go back home, that is to say to Mario's house, and stay there. Going out in this cold wasn't a good idea and I have to start looking after myself. I turn up the heat which was shut off in the night. Of all the houses I've lived in over the last few years I think this is the most comfortable. I gather and wash the mugs and cups I've left lying around, trying to maintain Mario's order as best I can. I try not to take any food into the bedroom and to put books back in their place on the shelf after I read them. I separate the rubbish into glass, paper, plastic and organic, I water the plants, and when it's necessary I'll vacuum the living room.

I should've given Mrs Takahashi all the money I had left so she could find a place and get in touch with her husband or whoever. I should never have brought her here. I try to think of something else, but the image of her on the river bank keeps coming back to me again and again. I look out the window, it looks like it's really cold outside. The few passers-by I see on the street are

121

covered up to their ears. I turn on the TV, the woman on the news says it's going to be a harsh winter, with freezing winds from the places she points to on the gigantic map of Germany. Afterwards they show images of demonstrations across several cities, students, human rights organizations and immigrants protesting the budget cuts for accepting refugees. A woman carrying a baby in her arms cries. I can't understand what she's saying. Images of the protestors are interspersed with shots of boats overflowing with people. The coast guard rescuing life rafts about to sink; men, women, and kids risking their lives to get to Europe. The reporter talks about the 800,000 asylum seekers this year alone.

I'm startled by a bang on the door. I turn off the TV. I freeze. It's Mrs Takahashi, I think, but she's not strong enough to bang like that. 'Who is it?' I call without getting up. I hear Miguel Javier's voice asking me to please open the door. I know it's him even though I've never heard him sound so serious, so grave, so determined. When I open the door he walks in without saying hello and strides into the middle of the living room. He doesn't look at me, he doesn't sit, his entire body seems to be repressing an urge to break everything in his path.

'Have you heard anything from my sister?' he says.

'Anything like what?' I ask.

'Have you talked to her, do you know where she is?'

I think back to our last phone call, count the days. 'We haven't talked in a while.'

'When was it you last talked? Where was she?'

'I don't know, it was a few days ago.'

The Tucumano's eyes are moist, he walks slowly to one end of the sofa and sits down. I infer that something bad has happened to Marta Paula, I remember now her anguished tone and two of the last sentences she said: 'It's because I went to Feli's that I'm like this. She did something to me.'

I sit at the other end of the sofa and stammer something about that last phone conversation. Miguel Javier stares at the floor while I talk.

'She's disappeared,' he interrupts. 'She hasn't been home for two days.'

I try to calm him down, I lean over to hug him but he pushes me away. 'She'll turn up soon,' I say.

I go and get Shanice's mobile phone and try to figure out exactly when I last talked to Marta Paula but the device is too sophisticated for me. I find messages I hadn't seen before. My hands sweat and I feel the phone slip.

'If something happened to her because she went to see that witch I swear I'll never forgive you.'

I dial the number she last called me from but no one answers. I didn't ask Marta Paula to go and see the psychic, but I could've tried to stop her. I was curious, I wanted to know what else she'd say about my pregnancy. The fact that the Tucumano was worried made me think that she was no charlatan but a real medium, someone with paranormal powers. Now his sister is missing and I can't stop thinking about what she said the last time we talked: *Feli did something to me*. Miguel Javier is pale. I offer him some tea and he accepts with a barely perceptible nod of the head. When I bring it to him he asks me not to leave him alone, says he's never been so frightened in his life. His anger seems to have faded.

'She'll show up,' I repeat.

Miguel starts to cry, and seeing him like that breaks my heart.

Once he calms down he tells me that his mother called two days ago to tell him that his sister hadn't come home the night before. Miguel, from ten thousand kilometres away, organised a search. His other sisters don't seem to have the time to give the issue the attention it deserves. The first thing he did was track down his former brother-in-law. Their relationship had never been very good so the interaction was cold and hostile and he didn't get any information out of him. He's worried about the kids, Marta Paula's children. His mother is looking after them but she's got too much on her plate to begin with. 'I have to go back,' he says, 'if she doesn't show up tonight I have to go back to Tucumán.'

Miguel Javier hasn't been to school in days, spending all his time making calls and writing e-mails. He even talked to the Tucumán police to tell them about Feli, about that place in the La Aguadita slum surrounded by black magic, prostitution, and drugs. He didn't really expect the police to do much but he felt better knowing a report had been filed.

We talk about how he'll get home tomorrow or the next day in the event that his sister is still missing. Miguel Javier can buy a ticket on his credit card and pay for it over the next few months with his scholarship money. It's exams time and his absence will mean a setback in his hard-earned academic achievement, but now's not the time to think about that. We sit at Mario's desk and search for flights to Buenos Aires and connections to Tucumán. There's an *Aerolíneas Argentinas* flight leaving from Frankfurt tomorrow at noon. If he takes the first train he could get to the airport in time. But I convince him to wait a little while, to spend the night here, checking in with his family in Tucumán. If there's no news after five in the morning he'll buy the ticket.

I cook sausages and potatoes and open one of the bottles of wine Mario has in the kitchen; I know he keeps them for special occasions but when I explain he'll understand. 'You can't drink,' the Tucumano tells me. We turn the conversation to my pregnancy and the change in subject makes us both feel better. I tell him that one glass won't hurt and he tells me that I look chubby. His eyes hover over my tits and thighs as he says it but then he immediately looks down into his glass. We also talk about the wine, neither of us is an expert on the matter but we agree that the one we're drinking is so nice that we'd really enjoy it if we weren't in such a terrible situation.

In a little while we'll call his mother's house again. Miguel Javier walks over to the window and motions for me to come quick.

'Is that snow that's falling?' he asks.

'Yes, it's snowing,' I confirm.

' *'sheautiful*, I've never seen snow,' he says pressing his face to the glass.

The sound of Shanice's mobile phone startles us. I imagine it's Joseph calling. I search for the phone between the couch cushions. I keep hearing the ring but I can't find it, thinking how I'll have to tell Joseph we can't see each other tonight. Finally I see the phone on one of the bookshelves and I run over to it. I answer before it cuts off.

'It's me, Marta Paula.'

'Marta Paula! Where are you?!'

'I'm staying in a hostel. I needed to be alone.'

'Are you okay?!'

'Yes.'

Miguel grabs the phone away from me. He shouts at her, asks over and over why she didn't let us know where she was. He asks if anyone had done anything to her. He asks if she's alone. He tells her that she's crazy, that she's totally irresponsible, that he was about to get on a plane to go looking for her, that he loves her a lot, that he couldn't carry on living if something bad happened to her.

I go into the kitchen so he can talk in private. I wash the dishes, I dry them, I dry my tears with the same tea towel. The brief cry seems to settle my nerves.

Miguel Javier comes into the kitchen and hands me the phone, he says that his sister wants to talk to me.

'You understand why I did it, don't you?'

'I think so, but you really scared us.'

'I needed to think.'

'Think about what?'

'To think about things, about my life. It was Feli who made me think about what I was doing with my life, and back home with the kids making such a racket all the time, I can't think. But it took me longer than I'd planned, it took me two days to think, but I'm going back home now.'

'Take care of yourself, Marta.'

'I will, you guys don't need to worry, tell my brother not to worry, that he needs to focus on graduating.'

'Okay, I send you a big hug.'

'Me too. Oh, I just remembered: when I went to Feli's the other day she told me you were having a girl. Congratulations.'

After Marta Paula hangs up, Miguel Javier and I talk for a while about his sister, about the snow and the wine and Mario. I'm dead tired and my eyes begin to close. 'It's time for me to go,' he says. We exchange a long hug at the door. Miguel walks away, huddled in his jacket, jumping up and down to catch the falling snowflakes, like a little boy.

# ELEVEN

## I

Last night after Miguel Javier left I called Joseph but he didn't pick up. I have the impression he's avoiding me so I won't try to get in touch with him again until he turns up on his own.

The snow fell heavily all morning. It's so cold that I sharpen my culinary creativity to avoid having to go out to get anything, I don't even change out of my pyjamas. I'll make the most of what I have: potatoes, instant soup mix, flour, sausages, tomatoes, and a bit of sliced meat. I watch TV all day, closely following the news of the refugees and the outbreaks of violence in a few European capitals. There are only a few images of the bombings in the Middle East, but it's enough to paint a picture of absolute disaster.

For the first time, I miss my family and friends in Buenos Aires.

I open Mario's boxes again and spread his photos,

letters and papers across the living room floor. I don't really know what I'm looking for but I find myself once again staring at the picture of the strange animals. Mario and I, both blurry, stand in a clearing in the woods outside Heidelberg; the city can be glimpsed between the trees in the distance. The animals look like miniature bison and they seem to be approaching us with caution. I don't remember anything about this day but I imagine that my dad must've taken the picture. I look at the photos of him; he smiles in all of them and I start to cry, wishing I could hug him one more time.

I look at the picture of Elvio, Mario's young boyfriend who disappeared. I find something about him unsettling but it takes me a moment to figure out what it is. I'm saddened, of course, when I think of his fate but this discomfort comes from something else. Elvio looks strikingly similar to Joseph. His large dark eyes, the wide smile, the thick black hair, heavy eyebrows, even his coat looks like the seventies trench coat that Joseph always wears.

I place the picture on a shelf so I can look at it from the sofa, the likeness at this distance is uncanny.

It's already getting dark, the day is over, an entire day of my life in which I didn't see or speak to anyone. Sleep comes over me before I can gather up Mario's mementos and I fall asleep on the sofa. I have fitful dreams of a little girl playing in a clearing in the woods. It could be me or it could be another little girl, it could be my daughter.

## II

The sound of keys in the lock wakes me up. Before I know it someone is inside. It's Mario. Through half-closed eyes I see him walk in with a suitcase which he sets down beside the sofa I'm lying on. It's morning and Mario smiles at me. 'You fell asleep down here,' he says. I look around at the mess of papers and photos, his papers and photos, his most intimate memories spread out on the rug.

'I'm sorry, I was looking at the pictures last night…'

'Don't worry about it, you can look at whatever you want. We'll put it away later.'

Mario looks well, really well. This immediately makes me happy. I'd imagined him on his last legs in some clinic in Frankfurt and now he's here and not only does he not look ill but he looks better than before. I ask him how he's doing and he says he's perfect. He asks me how I am, if I went back to the doctor, he says I look beautiful and I'm showing a lot more now. I heat up some coffee left over from the day before and I tell him about the episode with Mrs Takahashi, also about what happened with the Tucumano and his sister. Mario listens as if I were explaining the plot of a movie, he's highly entertained by the story but I think it's strange that he doesn't interrupt or say anything. When I finish he asks what else happened in the days he was gone. Nothing else, that's it, I lie. I don't have the guts to tell him about Joseph, I wouldn't know what to say or where to start or whether we still have a relationship at all.

Outside it's started snowing again and the little garden is covered in white. Mario says that we're going to have a great time together over the holidays. The holidays? Of course, I hadn't thought of that at all. Once again I think about everyone in Buenos Aires. The holidays are going to be nice, he says again, but first I'm taking another trip. Mario is sitting on a thesis panel at the University of Berlin, it will be a very short trip, 'a getaway'. He has to leave tomorrow so he's not even going to unpack, he says. And then, as I pick up the photos and papers off the floor, he says that he's going with Joseph.

'I invited him along and set up a meeting at a little Berlin gallery connected to the university. It's a great opportunity for him. He's very excited about it.'

I carefully place each photo in the box. I don't have the words to respond and my body feels like it weighs a ton.

## III

I know I won't be able to sleep tonight. I toss and turn in bed, I get up, I go to the kitchen. I drink an entire jug of water. Tonight, in this house, everything I know seems to have become very distant, unreachable. Mario sleeps in his room and tomorrow Joseph will come here to meet him. I imagine them arriving in Berlin, Joseph's smiling face, the smile that shows all his teeth and his glittering dark eyes. I imagine them stopping to eat at some restaurant before checking in to the hotel. I see Mario adjusting his glasses, moving his hands. The rest of the images that come to my mind are like something from a gay porn film, their naked bodies in a reddish light, their faces disfigured by pleasure. The scenes I imagine are so clichéd that I start to laugh. Mario and Joseph might not even share a room, I have no idea. I wouldn't dare ask so I should stop thinking about it.

I remember Mrs Takahashi and I feel terribly guilty. I'm not a good person, a good person wouldn't have done what I did. Because I know it was her wandering barefoot along the riverbank.

Trying not to make any noise that might wake Mario, I go to his desk and turn on the computer. In my inbox

1,472 unread messages have accumulated since I arrived in Germany. The majority of them are unimportant. I delete almost all of them, one by one without reading them. I stop at one from an old high school classmate. She talks about a reunion she's organizing that weekend. The e-mail is from almost two months ago. I imagine the reunion and what my former classmates might look like after so many years. I immediately remember the smell of jasmine outside the house I lived in as a teenager. I save the e-mail so I can respond and apologise for not going. I'll say that I would've loved to go but I'm in Europe.

I also save an e-mail from Santiago in which he tells me that Ringo died a month ago and he was a good dog right up to the end. He says it in three lines and he signs off coldly.

I don't even open the e-mails from my former co-workers.

I read a message from one of my father's former students. He sends a paper he wrote in homage to him. He talks about my father's contribution to philosophy but also about his sense of humour and the happy unity between his life and work. I read it several times.

There's an e-mail from Marta Paula written yesterday from a cyber café. She tells me about the unbearable heat in Tucumán and the commotion she stirred up in her family after spending two nights away from home.

I open an e-mail from my mum who still doesn't know about my pregnancy. She thinks I'm just travelling and meeting interesting people. She says I sounded strange the last times we talked on the phone. She asks what my plans are, if I'm going to keep travelling or if I already have a flight home. She says she's been feeling a bit depressed and that she isn't in the mood to do anything special for New Year's Eve. She says that if I'm coming back, we should take a trip out of town for Christmas.

I close my inbox and I see the *Aerolíneas Argentinas* website that Miguel Javier and I looked at the last time he was here. There are a few flights with seats available before the holidays. I type in my first and last name and my passport number, but the session times out before I get to the next step.

I fall asleep at the desk for a few minutes and wake up with a sore neck. I turn off the computer, too tired to think anymore. It's still night-time. I make it to bed and lie down. I don't know how much longer I'll stay in Heidelberg, but I do know that I'm going to sleep till noon. Mario will probably be gone before I wake up.

## IV

Joseph, sitting on the sofa where we lay together several times in recent days, doesn't say a word. He waits for Mario to get ready so they can leave. He just sits there with his arms crossed and a blank stare, looking bored. I feel like smacking him, throwing something at his head, pushing him out of the house. But I barely have the strength to approach him.

'You're not going to say anything to me?' I say looking him in the eye.

Joseph blinks, slowing raising and lowering his long lashes. He has a bag and a portfolio case that must contain his photography work. What right do I have to get angry, to feel betrayed? Joseph looks back at me, his mouth is so close to mine that it makes me tremble.

Mario appears, freshly showered and clean shaven. He looks happy, he tells us he hasn't been to Berlin in a long time, that this invitation was fortunate. As he gathers his things to leave he discovers the photo of Elvio on the bookshelf; I tell him, stuttering, that I forgot to put it back with the other pictures. He holds it in his hand for a few seconds and then puts it back on the shelf where I'd left it. He doesn't seem angry. Just the opposite, he says it's a better spot for that picture after so much time put away. Joseph still hasn't said anything, not even about his obvious similarity to Elvio. Neither of them seem to notice; or maybe they've talked about it so many times that it's stopped being something noteworthy.

Mario asks me to follow him to the kitchen and he shows me a jar full of money hidden among the pantry items. It's over five hundred euros, for expenses around the house or whatever I need, he says. That won't be necessary, I answer embarrassed, but he repeats that it's for whatever I need and he hugs me and I feel an affection so sincere that I'm moved to tears. Mario closes the kitchen door, I assume he's going to tell me something he doesn't want Joseph to hear.

'I didn't go to Frankfurt for work, I went to have surgery for a little tumour that they found. But it's nothing. Everything turned out fine.'

'Why didn't you tell me? Why didn't you let me go with you?'

'I didn't want to worry you in your state, and you already have enough problems... Everything turned out fine, just fine. But that picture of Elvio you left there made me think of something... something I have to ask you.'

'Of course, whatever you need.'

'If someday... if I die, whenever that may be, I want you to take my ashes to the La Plata forest and spread the ashes on the ground. You're the only person I can ask.'

Mario smiles, he seems embarrassed by the request. I promise to carry out his wishes. We're silent for a moment and then we laugh nervously. He opens the door and reminds me that he'll be back next week and that I shouldn't hesitate to use the money for whatever I need.

The taxi has arrived to take them to the station. Joseph says goodbye with a kiss on the cheek and I watch them get in the car talking happily about things I can't hear.

## V

My last days in Heidelberg were uneventful. The trees in the garden were completely covered in snow and I didn't go out at all until Friday, when there was nothing left in the kitchen and I had to go grocery shopping to keep from starving to death. I wrapped myself up tight and found a shovel to make a path through the snow piled up at the front door. I walked to the city centre, I bought fruit, vegetables, and bread. At a shop that sold Christmas decorations I bought some bright pink paper flowers that reminded me of Shanice. I decided to take them to the cemetery; I hadn't been back to visit her grave since the funeral.

A worker by the cemetery gates glanced at my groceries and said people weren't supposed to go in with food. I showed him the paper flowers and promised I would just be a minute. 'Just a minute then,' he repeated.

I retraced the path we took that morning with Shanice's parents and a few of the students. I set the flowers on the ground and noticed a picture of Shanice propped against her headstone. She looked to be about three or four years old and her parents were holding her hands. I left quickly, keeping my promise.

Once outside, I realised that I hadn't just wanted to visit Shanice but to look for clues about her mother. I'd spent days frightened she might pop up at any moment but also constantly worried and curious about her. If she'd gone back to Japan, if her husband had come to get her or if she was wandering around alone in this bitter cold. Then I crossed the street and I saw her. Mrs Takahashi was walking with her back to me in her long-sleeved black dress; there she was, safe and sound, moving away from the cemetery. My heart pounded. She'd managed to stay in Heidelberg. I felt the need to know where she'd been staying, what she'd been doing to survive all this time. I sped up so as not to lose sight of her and I followed at a prudent distance. I trailed her for many, many blocks. We passed luxury hotels and modest ones, at each one I thought she was going to stop but I was mistaken. She seemed to be going nowhere. Once we crossed the Neckar I no longer recognised the streets.

I noticed that the air had changed, that a cold wind had started up, carrying with it the smell of tea or burned wood. Lights began to turn on in the doorways as snow dripped slowly from the roofs.

I knew we were reaching the outskirts when the houses became more and more spaced out. The windows had their curtains drawn. A few minutes later there were no houses at all. I thought about turning back. I was still carrying my groceries which were beginning to get too heavy, but my curiosity was too great. When we reached the forest, Mrs Takahashi walked down a slope into the trees. I stopped. I recognised the place, I had the feeling I'd been there many times. I knew that at the bottom of the slope was the lake I used to visit with my father over thirty years ago. I walked a little further and confirmed that it was still there, in the middle of the woods, a frozen lake that looked exactly as it had in my childhood. I hadn't thought about the place in so many years but the memory came back, sharp and vivid: my father's blue coat, his warm hand holding mine, the two of us laughing, the smell of ice. I was so distracted by the memory that I lost sight of Mrs Takahashi. But she soon reappeared, crossing the lake with quick short steps. Her black silhouette stood out against the silvery reflections on the surface. When she got to the other side and disappeared among the trees, I stepped onto the ice. My shoes gripped well and I tried to imitate her short confident steps. I felt my lungs fill with the clean fresh air, and I convinced myself it had been a good idea to come here after so many days shut inside. But then I heard a noise, like a moan, a deep sigh that seemed to rise up from the bottom of the lake. I stood still, motionless. I wondered about the sound ice makes before it breaks up. There was no one else around. I saw an animal appear from between the trees and stop at the edge of the lake. It was hard to tell in the dim light but it looked like one of those goats or miniature bison from Mario's photo. I lowered my head and saw my reflection in the ice, my body larger and heavier than normal and still holding the two grocery bags. Very slowly, I lowered them, setting them down as far away from me as possible. I watched the fruit roll across the ice. Again I heard the moan from beneath my feet. I wished I knew the Hail Mary or any other prayer. I stood still for I don't know how long, shaking, until the sound stopped and I was able to move to solid ground. I took a few steps into the woods and collapsed on the snow. The animal I'd seen from the other side of the lake reappeared and slowly approached me. It was round, with short legs and two small horns sticking out of its flat forehead. It sniffed me and stared at me with its large wide-set eyes. It made a sound with its snout and leaned toward me. I knew that it wouldn't hurt me. I was lost, but I was safe. I took a deep breath and clutched the animal to me for warmth. Night fell.

We saw an owl fly from the top of a tree. We saw the clouds part, change shape, and disintegrate in the sky. We saw three other bison appear and watch us from far away.

My new friend stood up very slowly and joined the others. The four of them moved off into the trees. I wished I could stand up and find my way home. But I didn't have the strength yet. I lay on the ground for a while longer, looking up. The sky was completely clear and it began to fill with stars.